Scaring the Crows

21 Tales for Noon or Midnight

Gregory Miller

Illustrated by John Randall York

For Chuck!

I hope you enjoy these tales, both light and dark... Thanks so much for coming...

6/2/10
Monroeville

Stonegarden.net Publishing
http://www.stonegarden.net

Reading from a different angle.
California, USA

Scaring the Crows Copyright © 2009 Gregory Miller

ISBN: 1-60076-147-X

This is a work of fiction. Names, characters, places and incidents are products of the author's imagination or are used fictitiously and are not to be construed as real. Any resemblance to actual events, locales, organizations or persons, living or dead, is entirely coincidental.

> StoneGarden.net Publishing
> 3851 Cottonwood Dr.
> Danville, CA   94506

All rights reserved. Printed in the United States of America. No part of this book may be used or reproduced in any manner whatsoever without written permission, except in the case of brief quotations embodied in critical articles and reviews. For information address StoneGarden.net Publishing.

> First StoneGarden.net Publishing paperback printing:
> October 2009

> Visit StoneGarden.net Publishing on the web at
> http://www.stonegardenbooks.com

Cover art and design by John Randall York

"Steel" was first published in 'Rosebud,' issue 41 (Spring 2008)

"Without Power" was first published in the StoneGarden.net Publishing anthology "Don't Turn the Lights On."

For who else but Ray Bradbury

Table of Contents

Scaring the Crows	7
Big Plans	16
Stapleton's Dog	22
Goodbye, Friend	27
Without Power	31
Two Calls	38
The Hunt	43
Lorna Gould's Roses	51
Birthday	56
The Piano	62
Arachno	66
The Day After	77
Come Spring	81
Wolf Stone	86
All, Always	93
Steel	101
An Unknown Shore	106
A Sense of Duty	111
Welcome Home	125
Armistice Day	130
Hollow's End	134

Scaring the Crows

Edith Krepps had given up on men years ago, and now avoided them with a passion that bordered on obsession. Too many abuses, insults, lies and disappointments had left her barren of optimism for future relationships and possessive of a distrust and hatred for virility that gained ground with every passing day.

Anger, she constantly reminded herself. *I'm* angry. *I have a* right *to be angry*. And so she was.

Yet intermingled with her anger, at first subtly, now all too obviously, was something else.

She fought it heart, soul and mind. She reasoned against it. She raved at it. But as the flame of her anger burned more brightly, so also did…fear. Men scared her. *Terrified* her. Intellectually, she had come to understand her own inherent strength. She was self-sufficient, autonomous, and resourceful. She had a good brain on her shoulders and a strong body to support it. But she was…she was…

Oh, God. *Fear*ful.

Pittsburgh, home all her life, became unlivable. The close city streets contained too much to prey on her nerves. The source of her fear was everywhere: stopping by her walk with the mail, processing her groceries at the store, handing her change on the toll roads…

Even Edith's Family Diner, her one claim to critical and commercial success, had become an emotional liability. Dodging three dozen fears a block, she arrived at work every morning a frazzled, anxious wreck. Once there, she spent the rest of the day serving her apprehensions meatloaf, chicken and biscuits, corn soup, coleslaw, and burgers.

Have there always been this many in here? she wondered one day, surveying the patrons as her waitresses moved between them. Stifled by testosterone, Adam's apples, Y-chrome voice boxes and splayed-legged posturing, she closed up early that night, sold out, and retired at the age of forty-seven to the suburbs.

The suburbs, however, turned out no better than the city. Paternal households hemmed Edith in, keeping her up nights. Since the neighborhood rules precluded mailboxes, every morning the mailman *came to the door* and jammed letters through a slot. Once every few weeks a meter man prowled the bushes in the back yard.

Even Edith's nervous tics developed twitches. She began grinding her teeth in her sleep.

Then one day she noticed an ad in the paper for a rental house just an hour away, on the edge of a tiny town called Still Creek, population 1200. It was a fading town, dying because the coal mines were dead, the men who worked them having black dust-coughed themselves into early graves decades before.

It was a quiet town. Isolated.

Perfect.

The house was large. It stood on the other side of a hill at the end of Still Creek's last street. Beyond it, before it, and on both sides? Corn fields. The mailbox was at the end of a dirt lane over two hundred yards from the house.

Also perfect.

She rented a moving van, loaded everything up herself, drove it to Still Creek, unloaded everything herself, took a brief look round the property, locked the door tight, and basked in the absence of clammy hands, creeping flesh, pounding heart, and nauseous stomach.

Life, for the first time in several years, was finally good.

* * * * *

The feeling was like a wet, ice-cold finger twisting in her ear.

In the back yard garden, Edith looked up sharply, pulling off her dirt-caked gloves and letting them fall in the lettuce.

She stood up slowly, peering carefully at the unshuttered house, the dustbowl driveway.

Nothing.

Nothing at all but the dread, three months gone but now returned, seethed through her veins in numbing pulses.

She turned with a gasp in a quick, tight half-circle, eyeing everything.

Knee-high corn stalks rustled in a warm, gentle breeze.

The weathervane rooster atop the house twisted, creaking, to face east.

A man was standing in the field, staring at her.

Even as she screamed, Edith took in his patched blue jean overalls, his red and black checkered shirt, his frayed rope belt and black-knit gloves. Her eyes moved up his body, dilated pupils capturing his tattered, wide-brimmed straw hat, his lolling neck, his mottled…

She squinted in the sun and took a step closer, then two, three, ten.

A man? Clothes rippling in the wind but no body movement? Arms spread messianically against a wooden pole?

A man? Straw sticking out of the shirt? A ceramic jack o' lantern for a head?

The scarecrow grinned at her stupidly. Edith breathed a long, shaky sigh of relief.

But where had it come from? It hadn't been there yesterday, or even earlier that morning, and she hadn't been away from the house all day. Edith had made it clear to her landlady, Mrs. Amos, that *no one* was to set foot on the property without prior warning via telephone. No one had called, and beyond that, she should have seen a work truck or heard the pounding of the scarecrow post as it was knocked into the earth.

She went back inside and called Mrs. Amos, but her son answered instead.

"She's in Florida for the next six weeks. Needs the time off and doesn't want bothered. Her blood pressure, you know. What can I do for you?"

But Edith, gasping for air, her very bones chilled, had already slammed down the phone with a heavy *clunk*.

Fine, then. The police!…But in this district? Men, all of them…

Trespasser or no, she would have to make do alone.

* * * * *

As the green fields of rustling corn ripened, yellow shocks and seedling strands waving in hot, late-morning summer wind, Edith woke unrefreshed, unfulfilled by sleep, bothered by the lingering obsessions of one AM, two AM, three AM, four. There had been no sign of any outsiders on her property since the appearance of the scarecrow, but the nagging sense of insecurity still plagued her.

Why? she demanded. *No one in the house, no one on the property. No one in sight.*

But…

But there was, really.

After the sixteenth restless night had passed, at last, into pale morning, Edith went downstairs and made a pot of strong hazelnut coffee. As she ground the beans she happened to glance out the kitchen window, her gaze quickly drawn to the ragged effigy splayed upright in the field beyond the yard.

She shivered, then slowly looked down at her gooseflesh, pressed a hand to her quivering, bloodless lips, and tapped a finger to the racing pulse in her clammy wrist.

"Ridiculous!" she proclaimed. "Beyond ridiculous!"

Really? Is it really?

The scarecrow's clothes, build, presence. Her clacking teeth, cold veins, burning trepidation. The looming sense of dread. The unfounded, pervasive sense of constant invasion; of being watched, scrutinized….

A scarecrow? Yes.

Only a scarecrow?

"Only a scarecrow, yes…but *male*."

Ignore it, she thought. *Ignore*. To be afraid of the living is one thing. That fear, however irrational, had a foundation in her life. To be afraid of the dead? A little more abstract, but she could understand it. But fear of dried corn stalks and an old farmer's hand-me-downs? That was a fear which needed to be put down, knocked away, cast off and forgotten. Killed.

Go on out, now. Ignore it. Go tend the garden.

"Damn it," said Edith a week later, peering from behind lace curtains at the dead plants gone back to soil.

* * * * *

It was the following day, in the calm, humid warmth following a brief summer storm, that Edith noticed the change.

The scarecrow was gone.

Gone! Knowing it was in the field was bad enough. Somehow, not knowing where it was struck her as far worse.

Taken? Knocked off the pole by wind? Battered down by rain?

She went to her bedroom on the second floor and looked out the window. Peering down from that angle she could see the empty bamboo pole clearly. Straw hands, wet colored cloth and a ceramic pumpkin skull lay in a tangle several feet away among the corn stalks.

"Fine," she assured herself. "That's fine."

But the next day wasn't so fine.

"If I didn't know better," Edith said, looking out the window for the two-dozenth time in as many hours. She closed her mouth with a clatter of enamel.

Days passed.

An inch. A foot. A yard. Ever so slowly, but without a doubt, the scarecrow was closing in on the house.

"A trick of the light," Edith said. "Wind. An animal. Kids."

At first she believed it, yet the sunlight and moonlight were steady and played no tricks. The air was muggy and calm. There was no evidence of dogs or other large animals on her property. Besides, what animal would return night after night to nudge, prod, pull—just enough to scare? Teenagers? They never bothered her, preferring the intrigue of woods or the troubles of parties far out in the countryside to the boring, cultivated fields around her end of town.

The chair dragged up from the kitchen became a fixture by her bedroom window. By turn, so did Edith. Downstairs existed in dimness and dark, the curtains pulled across the windows, the doors latched, bolted, and reinforced by stools lodged firmly under knobs. She wanted to leave town but could not; beyond Still Creek prowled fears she could not face. Even the progress of the straw man scared her less than them.

It did, however, scare her very, very much.

September came, autumn on its heels. The scarecrow reached the edge of the cornfield.

That morning, waking from a short, troubled doze in her chair, Edith's tired, glazed eyes slowly focused. She leaned toward the frost-paned window, found the subject of her constant attention, and stared at it for a long moment before jumping up, skin seething with shock-sweat.

Colin!

A high school boyfriend came crashing into her mind, dredged up from deep, lost years: his thick neck, wrestler's arms, and close-cropped brown hair; his strangely high-pitched giggle when they watched *All in the Family* on Tuesday nights; his haughty stride, ridiculous posturing and constant primping; his overbearing smile when he announced that, yes, he *was* too good for her now, it *was* time to move on, his parents *didn't* approve, she came from the *wrong side of the tracks*; and last but not least, the way he'd swung his Number 28 Martinsville Mariners varsity jacket over his right shoulder as he'd walked away from her for the last time.

"Now how," she asked the scarecrow, "did you get that?"

Instead of the red and black woolen shirt, the scarecrow now sported a tight-fitting denim Martinsville Mariners varsity jacket, Number 28.

She took two Quaaludes and slept for twelve hours.

When Edith woke up, she sighed with relief. The jacket was gone, the old weather-stained shirt back in place. It was the same—

"Wait. Wait."

Penny loafers.

"Bernard Renfrew." A no-show at Senior Prom. But the day before that horrible night, he'd left those shoes at her house, part of a rented tuxedo outfit that had been used to charm and impress— not her, but a close friend instead. She had fed them to Flower, her purebred German Shepherd. Now they adorned the scarecrow's husk feet, looking decidedly out of place.

And the scarecrow itself was unquestionably closer.

From then on, every time she turned away, slept, ate, scratched herself over the next few days and nights, the scarecrow gained ground … and not only that, *changed*.

David Palchak. Nick Miller. Lloyd Stackhouse.

It was peeking through the last corn stalks, face down, arms splayed out before it, its left wrist sporting a gold Rolex that gave Edith shudders of memory.

Ryan Nelson. Wallace Goodwin. Jason Knapik.

It lay among tomato husks in the abandoned garden, a thin silver necklace she had bought for Brian Caldwell, the first man who ever punched her in the face, around its corn stock neck.

Stuart Baumgarten. Peter Wendell. Marty Bainbridge.

It sat propped against the peeling red picnic table under the maple tree, a gold and amber ring lodged on a twisted, dry grass finger that dredged up memories of a high-society penthouse, two defense attorneys, and drugged drinks.

Lester Ringwold. Richard Brummett. Burt Winger.

It lay six feet from the back porch door, and on its grinning, hollow head a dark smudge in the shape of her ex-husband's birthmark reminded her of three years she had spent the previous decade trying hard to forget...

Palpitations plagued her.

Blood thudded in bright red ears.

Breathing grew difficult.

Then, finally, *finally*:

"Enough!"

After days of watching, silent, hungry, scared, Edith leapt to her feet. "Pitiful. *Pitiful!* You're a failed businessman now! Your second wife left you! Your son hates you! Six months in jail for a third DUI! *How did that feel?* You're nothing! Broken! *You're nothing at all!*"

Triumphant, she grinned. Then, still smiling toothily, she let darkness come. Her eyes rolled back in her head, the world went muddy, and her body ran like water to the floor.

* * * * *

Numberless hours of dreamless rest plus something Edith couldn't later put into words rose to nullify seventy-two hours of sleepless vigil and left her feeling oddly refreshed as cold night fell, veiling the house and yard in long shadows.

Words fell from her lips: "He was the last." Again: "He was the last."

She got unsteadily to her feet, leaned against the chair for support, and pressed the fingertips of her right hand to the cool glass of the window.

She looked out.

The scarecrow was gone.

Taking a deep breath, running a hand through her matted brown tangle of hair, Edith stood, head cocked, listening intently to the sighing of the house. The tension of her weight creaked the floor timbers. A pine branch scratched gently against the tin gutter pipe on the roof.

Down below, in the dark, something rustled.

Edith went to the edge of the stairs and peered into the black.

"You were a hundred and one people, and now all that's left is… you. That's my bet."

The darkness listened.

Edith hesitated a moment, then started downstairs.

The hallway was black, the arched entryway to the living room a yawning mouth. In the living room something whispered too softly to be understood.

Creaking across the old wooden floor beams, feeling her way carefully in the dark, Edith paused at the entryway.

"One by one I relived my failures through your clothes, my pains through your face. You tested me, and ... I survived. I *survived*." She sounded surprised, and realized she was. She was also very calm. "And what's left is ... what? Straw and stick, corn cob and grass. Leaf and wire. Am I right?"

The silence was noncommittal.

"No, more than that, of course. You walk. You watch. You wait. But harmless. Defenseless. Easily burnt, broken, withered. Easily mildewed and rotted. More than that, very cold. And perhaps... lonely?"

The assent came, and it was a corn-shuck voice, a reedy rasp that spoke around the fumblings of field insects and clods of cool mud.

"I must admit," she continued, "it has been a *very* long time since I last had a man in my home—of *any* kind," she added hastily. "I'd like to take it slow. Maybe we could just... talk?"

Yes, the voice said, talking would be fine. *Just* fine. Come in. Sit down.

"Oh yes," Edith said, stepping into the living room's waiting dark.

She felt her way to the couch and sat down at one end. She could feel the weight of something else on the other. She cleared her throat.

"I think maybe we should have a little light. That's only proper. A little light?" she asked.

Yes.

"Okay," she said, and flicked a switch.

Edith looked at what was sitting beside her on the couch... and *winked*.

Big Plans

He laid his new tie and freshly pressed shirt on the dresser. He took his sports coat from the closet and whisked it down before giving his new loafers a final polish.

"Ben," said Cathy, looking sleepily over at him from the bed.

"What, hon?"

"It's five in the morning. Your interview isn't until nine and it only takes an hour to get to the city."

"You never know about Pittsburgh traffic," said Ben, adjusting his tie. "And there's construction on 76 … How's the hair? I think Ross cut it too short."

"Fine as always."

He ran his fingers through it, unconvinced.

"Now how is it?"

Cathy rolled her eyes. "*Still* fine … as always. I should get up and make you breakfast."

"No, not a chance. I didn't mean to wake you up. Go back to sleep."

She shook her head. "This is an important day. You need to eat."

"I can make myself something."

"You need something more than just *cereal*."

Downstairs in the kitchen, Cathy tended the bacon while Ben stared out the window, a folded *Still Creek Gazette* untouched by his elbow.

"You don't need to be nervous," she said, forking the bacon onto a paper towel and blotting out the grease. "You said you already got the job. It's just a formality."

"I know. But the superintendent will be there. I've never met her before. And both principals this time. And the head of the English department. And there *are* two other candidates. If I blow it, they're waiting in the wings."

"That won't happen."

Cathy handed over Ben's breakfast and took a seat beside him.

"Tell me again what we'll do with the money," she said.

Ben sipped his coffee and allowed a smile. "We'll pay off all our loans. We'll sell the house and move to Penn Hills, just ten minutes from the heart of the city. We'll see shows and eat at a different restaurant every Saturday night. Then we'll find three, maybe four restaurants that we really like and we'll only go to those. The waiters and waitresses will learn our names. We'll be regulars. And every Christmas our families will drive out from the country and we'll take them to Pine Forest to see the light display—the biggest in Pennsylvania. And I'll teach thirty years' worth of students and attend seminars downtown every summer. And you'll become head librarian at Carnegie University, or maybe Pitt. And every August before school starts up again we'll fly somewhere different for vacation."

Cathy smiled. "Every time you say it, you add something new. There's no need to *fly* somewhere for vacation every year. Driving is just fine."

Ben shook his head. "Well, maybe *sometimes* we'll drive. But I'm sick of Harrisburg and Gettysburg and Baltimore and Washington D.C. I want Los Angeles and Chicago and Denver and Seattle. I want London and Paris and Rome!"

"You've got egg on your tie."

Ben sighed and brushed it off.

Cathy kissed his cheek as he stood to go. "Drive safe. Take deep breaths. Pop a mint before you start to talk. And watch out for that nervous twitch. Remember that, and you'll do *fine*."

Two hours later, she picked up the telephone with a tremulous hand.

"I did fine," Ben told her.

* * * * *

She walked the three blocks to Stockton's Grocery and spent twenty-two dollars before returning home laden with brown paper bags. She spent half an hour on the telephone.

The small house they had shared for three years quickly filled with family and friends. There was a steady hum of life like bees in a hive, all bustle and work and business and laughter. Good smells wafted out from the kitchen and balloons bumped the ceiling in the dining room. Warmth saturated the living room, fogging the windows and hiding the cold outside.

"There's so much else we'll be able to do," Cathy told her mother. "So many new opportunities. So many new chances."

Her mother kneaded piecrust in a tin pan and smiled without looking up.

"Big fish in a small pond, is that it? And Pittsburgh's the ocean?"

Cathy nodded. "No more debt. No more small, crowded rooms and second-hand furniture. No more leaky ceiling or rusted-out shed. All our lives, and now we're moving out. That's how it should be. That's how it's supposed to happen."

"It's awful far."

She gazed at her mother for a long time. "Not so far," she said. "Not so far. You and Daddy will come visit and spent weekends with us."

Her mother smiled again. Still, she did not look up. "Yes," she said, and patted her hand. "Yes, that will be fine. It's a wonderful chance. We're all very proud of you."

Shortly before six, they heard Ben's car rasp into the driveway and everyone fell silent.

"Here he comes," Cathy whispered. The house hummed with hidden life.

As they waited, she looked around at the still, expectant faces. She smiled. Then, unexpectedly, the smile fell away, but it came back when Ben unlocked the door and stepped inside.

The wind had flushed his cheeks and blown his hair into a mess of bangs. His eyes, so often red and tired at the end of the day, now twinkled with pent-up joy. The tilt of his mouth spoke of triumph. Before he could take another step, a benign flood of people bore him up and into the house.

"Congratulations!" everyone cried. "Congratulations!"

And when, an hour later, the phone rang and Ben answered it, no one thought to ask who it was. Well into the evening they celebrated. Cake and ice cream and beer and songs. Stories and future plans. Back-slaps and bear hugs. Ben stayed in the middle of it all, laughing loudest, telling the tallest tales, eating and drinking and taking all good wishes with a toothy smile. And if he looked a little tired now and then, who could blame him? It had been a long day.

When the last of the friends left with the last of the family, they shut the door and stared at the litter scattered about the empty house. The smile fell from Ben's face along with his color. His shoulders slumped. Cathy watched as he trudged up the stairs without another word, and it was only then that she remembered the phone call and realized what it meant.

* * * * *

He lay in the dark on the bed, above the blankets, shoes still on. Outside, wind beat against the frost-rimmed windowpanes and shook the eaves. The air felt thin and cold. The night was thick.

Cathy crossed over to the bed and stared down at the darker shadow of her husband. She could hear his breathing. It was even but hard.

She sat down beside him and did not speak.

"It was an issue of clearances," he said at last. "That DUI when I was nineteen. They didn't know about that. I didn't even think to mention it. Here it doesn't matter so much, but there it does. I'll never be a teacher in the city."

More breathing in the darkness. Cathy's respiration found Ben's rhythm and joined it, chest pacing chest.

"There will be other jobs," she said. "Other opportunities."

"Not like that one," he replied. "Not like that."

She lay back on the bed, hair nestled beneath her head on the pillow. The mattress ebbed and flowed with their breathing, a living thing.

"I wanted to give us something we never had before," Ben said softly.

"I know. But then again, I'm not as upset as I thought I would be. Strange."

A sharp movement, and Cathy knew Ben had sat up and was looking at her.

"Tell me," he said slowly, "what we would have done with all that money."

Her eyes adjusted to the darkness and she stared up at the ceiling slats. "We would have paid off our loans," she began slowly. "Then we would have sold our house here and moved to North Hills, just ten minutes from the heart of the city. We would have seen shows and eaten at a different restaurant every Saturday night."

Ben was very quiet beside her, still looking at her through the dark. She could see him faintly now.

She continued, "Then we would have grown lonely and wondered why we had decided to move. We would have missed our family and friends. We would have missed the walks around town that we had once thought we would never miss. We would have invited everyone over for Christmas, but it wouldn't have been the same. And each year fewer and fewer people would have come. And so, after ten years, we would have moved back here, to this town that's small but *not* dying, and I would have taken my old job back as the Still Creek Elementary School assistant librarian, and you would have taken your old job back as a Still Creek High School English teacher. And we would have been very happy at long last."

She felt the bed creak as Ben lay back down. A hand found hers.

A gust of wind rattled the storm windows, bringing with it a spray of late-season ice that clattered against the glass and aluminum siding.

Inside, the room had grown very warm.

Cathy sat up and flicked on the light. She stood quietly at the edge of the bed.

"Please get up," she said.

"What?"

"Get up. Put on your coat."

Ben got up, looked around the room, looked into her face and then went to the closet and took out his coat and put it on. He sensed, rather than knew, that now was not the time for questions.

"Follow me," she said.

Cathy went ahead of him, down the stairs and, after hesitating, he followed.

As they reached the front door she opened it and said, "Outside."

"What?"

"Just step out."

Ben stepped out the door and she followed, shutting it behind them. They were out in the night.

"What are we doing?" he asked.

"Why, it's May 17."

"That date," he said. "It's very familiar."

Cathy nodded. "Three years ago today, we moved into this house. Here." She handed him a key.

He looked at it for a long moment, then recognized what it was for. He put it in the front door lock, turned it, and the door drifted open.

Cathy stepped in, turned, and said, "Come on. It's the first day."

Ben smiled as he followed.

Stapleton's Dog

The sullen wasteland spread out toward the overcast horizon.

They stared at it with approval. Around them, a cold wind carried with it a colder mist, and the mournful cry of a bird they did not recognize echoed through the desolation. October, that most melancholy of months, seemed highly concentrated in the 280 square miles of dead bracken, rotting vegetation, slimy moss, standing water, and quicksand.

"The greatest of the Dartmoor bogs!" exclaimed Tom Worthington, breathing in deeply. "Here we are."

"I wonder if it's as dangerous as the great Grimpen Mire." Stella, his wife of twenty-one years, rubbed her hands together to kill the chill. Even so, the flush in her cheeks wasn't just from the cold. She was excited, Tom noted. She was happy to be here. *Thrilled.*

"I'm sure it is," said Tom, scanning the distance. "I don't think Sir Arthur exaggerated his source."

Fourteen-year members of the Sherlock Holmes Society, they had been planning this visit for over a decade. Money was tight, but Tom's prompting had gradually won Stella over, and here they finally were. Both smiled as they took a few tentative steps closer to the bog's edge. Behind them the windows of the Gifford Bed & Breakfast glowed with light that promised warmth, food, and hot baths. Beneath their feet a fine, manicured lawn pushed away wildness with promises of croquet, picnics, and long walks on well-tended paths.

Neither of them paid any of that any mind. Their hearts were already caught in the mire.

"Doyle walked here," Stella said, nodding to herself. "On this very yard. On these very moors. In that very marsh."

"And now, so will we." Tom smiled.

"So many years of saving, and here we are, where *he* was," Stella went on. "And where he was is where Dr. Mortimer, Stapleton, Mr. and Mrs. Barrymore, Sir Henry, and dear old Watson and Mr. Sherlock Holmes himself *still* roam."

She reached into a coat pocket and withdrew a battered paperback. On the front cover a snarling, demonic hound glared out with fearsome red eyes.

"Yes, dear," said Tom. "You're absolutely right."

"I've always dreamed of standing in this spot with this book in my hand ... with you."

"For a while, it looked like that would never happen."

Stella glanced at Tom sharply. "I know. But that's over now. It's forgotten ... Ancient history! I hardly remember his face." She grasped his warm hands tightly. He noted that hers were very cold.

"That's good to know," Tom said evenly.

Stella stared at him a moment longer, then took a deep breath. In the time it took her to exhale, she had cheered again.

"Well, what say we explore a little?"

"Certainly," said Tom. "Where shall we go first?"

"The mire, of course!"

She took six steps forward along what looked like a solid, mossy path. For a moment it held. Then the earth sucked, shifted, and gave way. Mud lapped at her heels, encircling them in a tight, clammy grip. She fell sideways. A heartbeat later she was knee-deep in stinking brown muck.

"Help me, Tom!"

A curse, a wallowing splash, a desperate heave, and soon Stella lay safe on the lawn, breathing hard. Tom, also drenched, drew in a ragged breath and laughed.

"What's so funny?" Stella snapped, still gasping.

"I was just imagining the pony that Stapleton and Watson watched…The one that sank, screaming, to its death."

"I don't think that's very funny at all. It was a horrible scene. Doyle used it to provoke a sense of foreboding and foreshadowing in the reader, and he succeeded."

"And what did Stapleton say about the great Grimpen Mire when describing it to Watson?"

Stella sighed, delved into her pocket for the paperback, flipped a few pages, and quoted, "'Even in dry seasons it is a danger to cross it, but after these autumn rains it is an awful place.' Fine, fine. I see your point. I should have known better."

Tom grinned. "And *then* what does Stapleton say?"

More thin pages flipping. "Um… 'And yet I can find my way to the very heart of it and return alive.'"

"Yes!"

"I get it, Tom. All very clever."

"No, no. Don't be angry. Here."

He reached down and hoisted Stella to her feet. He dusted her off, removed a strand of slime from her hair, and smiled.

"Now for the surprise," he said.

"What surprise?"

"Did the water slop into your boots?"

"No. Good thing I wore the high tops."

"Excellent. Allow me."

Tom took Stella's hand and led her forward. For a moment he thought she would hold back, but she followed him, even after her near miss. Whistling, he stepped, without hesitation, twenty feet into the mire without so much as a squelch…Stella right behind.

"Tom! How—"

"Nothing at all!" He bowed.

"But—"

"Oh, I did my homework. Corresponded with some of the locals and took notes. Got a map. Studied it. And here we are. And here we go!"

He led the way again, slowly but steadily, and when they stopped a second time the green grass of the lawn looked very far away.

Stella could barely control her excitement. "I never imagined! It's … It's *wonderful*. Just like I thought it would be. How completely desolate! How horribly oppressive! Oh, Tom," she said, kissing him briefly on the cheek, "how can I ever *thank* you?"

"Oh, I'll think of something," Tom said. "But it's my pleasure. My way of saying, 'I want to start over.'"

Stella hugged him tight. "But how much farther are we going? It's getting dark."

"A ways yet," Tom said. "See that low hill?"

"What, way out there?"

"It's really more of an island. We'll walk out, take a look around, then head back for dinner."

They moved on, Tom picking his way carefully, Stella following in his footsteps. At last, with the faded sun sinking into the heart of the mire, they reached the hill.

"It really *is* more of an island," Stella said.

"Yes," said Tom, climbing up the low rise to where two long stones jutted up like fangs. "See?"

Stella nodded.

"And you know something?" Tom asked.

"What's that?"

"This is the very spot that inspired Doyle's description."

Stella shook her head. "Description of what? The marsh?"

"No. The place where the demon hound tore out Sir Hugo Baskerville's throat."

"Really?" Stella shuddered. She reached out and took Tom's hand.

Despite the chill, his palm was very warm… so warm that she let go of it very quickly.

"Really," Tom said, then paused. "It *is* all very impressive, isn't it? Just the way we pictured it?"

"Yes," said Stella, but now her tone was low, somewhat distracted. The wind had grown very strong and very cold. Dead rushes moaned and sighed. She shivered.

"Bow-wow," said Tom.

She blinked, uttering a startled giggle. "What?"

And then he pounced.

Goodbye, Friend

The call came at five o' clock, barely an hour after Adam Mitchell's last class of the day. He was still cold from the long walk across campus, and Dr. Robinson's voice, booming out thoughts on Roman philosophy, remained a close memory.

He sat down on his dorm cot and answered the phone.

"Adam?"

"Hi, Dad."

"Tank is bad."

"How bad?"

"You should come home. Mom says the vet can see him within the hour."

Adam took a deep breath. "I'll be there in twenty minutes," he said.

* * * * *

Tank lay in his kennel, breathing hard and staring straight ahead with cataract-stricken eyes that, even with limited vision, looked out at nothing anyone else could see. His lungs rasped and his chest heaved, over and over, and all the concentration he could muster was focused inward, oblivious to anything outside of his stricken body.

Adam knelt beside Tank and touched the long mane of hair on his neck.

"You remember what the vet said," Adam's father murmured.

"Yes, I remember."

"Will you do it?"

Adam paused. "I … I don't know. I'll see what the vet says this time."

His father sighed. "Tank has arthritis and cataracts, seizures and incontinence, all on top of his lung problems."

"I know."

"You need to do what's right."

Adam eased Tank out of his kennel and lifted him in his arms. "Right now, all I need is some help getting Tank out to the car," he said.

* * * * *

The late-November day turned cold as the sun went down, the afternoon rain to ice, and the headlights of passing cars dazzled off the foggy windshield and cast halos into Adam's eyes.

He kept one hand on the steering wheel, one hand on Tank's chest. The dog lay beside him on the passenger seat, wheezing softly.

"Easy now," Adam said. "Easy."

The vet's office was twelve long miles away, at the end of a complicated gauntlet of back roads and congested highway. Adam already felt frustration toward it. Every time the brake grated down, Tank grunted. Every time he took a turn too tight, Tank whined.

"Easy now," Adam said again.

Norle Street flashed by on his right, a brief glimpse of sign and dark road in the cold, driving sleet. As a child he had lived on that street, second house on the left. The memories of that time were all sunlight, sieved through age and years so only a vague feeling of childhood wonder remained—wonder at how the world worked, and especially how anything could ever change.

He looked down at the passenger seat and the memory of a long-gone Sunday morning came unbidden and unexpected. In that now-dark house, when he was five, he had looked at Tank and thought, "When I am twenty, he will be fifteen. When I am twenty-five, he will be dead." The idea had appalled him—that this young bundle, a reflection of himself, would die of old age long, long before he even knew full maturity—and he had taken comfort in the fact that such a time was so far in the future it might as well not exist.

But now it was close, and that other day, long ago in bright summer sunlight, felt faint and distant.

"Easy now," he said, patting Tank's neck. "Easy."

* * * * *

The turn came swiftly and caught him unaware. Tank fell sideways off the seat. Adam's open backpack vomited books onto the floor. Tires squealed and gravel crunched. The car lurched to a halt.

Adam took a deep breath, reached down, and lifted Tank back onto the seat. Tank whined softly.

"I'm sorry," he said, stroking his fur, but Tank did not look at him. For a week he had not looked at anyone.

"We'll get you fixed up and take you back home," he continued. "You'd like that, wouldn't you? To go home?" Once Tank had calmed, Adam reached into the back seat and picked up all the books. Absently, he glanced at a highlighted line from his Philosophy 121 textbook:

Never injure a friend, even in jest.
--Cicero

He paused, eyes frozen on seven words written by a man two thousand years silent who had found his voice again here, now, in a car at the side of a sleet-slicked road on a cold November evening.

He dropped the book and turned back to Tank. Tank, who had waited on the front porch every afternoon for him to return from school; who had kept vigil by his bed at night when he was sick; who had always, always put him first—unconditionally and without exception.

Never injure a friend, even in jest.

He started the car and pulled back onto the road, tears welling in his eyes. The whole time he kept his right hand on Tank, feeling the ebb and flow of the dog's belabored breath. He knew what he had to do.

Tank wouldn't be coming home.

Minutes passed slowly but inexorably. Twilight turned to night. Sleet turned to snow.

"You always put me first," Adam murmured.

As the lights of the veterinary clinic dotted the dark surrounding woods, Tank raised his head and licked Adam's hand.

Adam pulled into a parking space and turned off the car.

He looked down. Something had changed.

Never injure a friend…

He placed a trembling hand on Tank's cooling head, then on his still, silent chest. He closed Tank's eyes, then his own.

Without Power

Night came, and Rachel Phillips looked toward the ceiling. Darkness met her gaze and she saw nothing beyond it. The nothing scared her.

Her small hands clasped the corners of the quilt until her pudgy fingers went white in the knuckles. Far away, in the cold outside, a dog barked. She counted the barks until they numbered thirteen. Then the barks stopped abruptly, with a yelp.

Downstairs, no reassuring sounds came from the kitchen, the living room, the study or porch. In the other bedrooms no one spoke, snored, rustled blankets or fluffed pillows. She couldn't see the sliver of light that usually filtered under her door from the open bathroom. The back porch light didn't shine through the window.

The house was old. Once she'd asked Grandpa how old, and he'd said, "Older than you and me and your parents put together." That, she knew, was pretty old. In the past it was always warm and bright. Before two days ago. Before the sudden, cold-sweat drive through the snow and the quiet talk of hospitals from the front seat.

In the past it hadn't bothered her; the age hadn't been an issue and neither had the creaks and groans, the thumps and bumps, the far off murmurs and nearby squeaks.

Now they bothered her.

Now they kept her up, shivering, although February was stuck outside and the room was warm. Now they made her think of the dark fields beyond the edge of the back yard, past the picnic table and the maple tree; and of the forest; and of the church and graveyard past the fairgrounds. And of the carpets still stained with mud from the paramedics' shoes.

And it was now, with everything dark and everyone gone, that she realized something—something very *close*—was wrong.

"It's just the dark," Mommy would have told her. "We'll keep the bathroom light on."

But Mommy was out, and Daddy was out, and Grandma and Uncle John were out, and Grandpa—

Under the bed something rustled.

A mouse, Grandpa would have said. And she would have believed him because it would have been true.

Now, though.

Now.

The rustling continued, and Rachel moved to the center of the bed, arms and legs tucked up tight around her. Her lower lip began to quiver.

Whatever it was, it was more than a mouse. Bigger. The wooden floor creaked beneath its weight as it shifted, scuttling across the cool beams then back again.

She wanted to scream. She wanted to holler, reach out a hand, slap on a light switch. But no one was home and the power was out.

"Stay in bed," Daddy had told her. "We'll be back before eleven, and I want you asleep by then."

"But I want to come too."

"Tomorrow. You'll see him tomorrow."

No way to tell what time it was now. It had been 9:30 the last time she checked, before everything went dark. She would have to wait for the tolling of the church bell.

The bed lurched, bumped from below. A shriek escaped her lips. She clapped a hand to her mouth, eyes wide and staring.

Instead of counting seconds, she counted the pounding beat of her heart. She soon lost track, distracted by the smell and texture of the quilt against her nose and face. She held it there, over her, knees pulled up to her chest. The quilt would protect her. It always had.

But it's just a quilt, a small voice whispered.

"No," she whispered back.

Yet she knew it was true. If whatever lurked under her bed chose, it could slide out, rise up, and grab her, quilt and all. She would be spider's prey already wrapped in silk, ready to be consumed.

Now her imagination, already heated from overwork, kicked into overdrive. Images flashed across her mental vision, captivating her the way a gruesome accident captivates those who drive by it—unharmed, but cognizant of the fact that the blood on the road isn't syrup dyed red, that the teddy bear in the dirt isn't a prop, that the broken bodies aren't dummies.

A rabid dog with glowing green eyes lay in wait, drooling white foam.

Her first cousin, killed in a barn fire four years back, had come home again, pallid eyes gleaming from a charcoal-black face, clothes smelling of cinders.

A giant rat had raced up through the sewer, through the heating ducts, and was clawing at the grate in the wall, yellow teeth grown long and crooked, red gums dotted gray with disease.

The huge salamander she'd hooked with Grandpa when she was six had somehow survived. She remembered its gasping, toothless mouth, how it had lunged up at her when she reeled it in, its slimy body squirming and wriggling until, with a moan, it gurgled and stilled. And now it was back.

Or—

Or…

No.
She sniffed the air.
No. None of those.
She forced herself calm.
None of them.
Breathe in, out. Deep, slow breaths. In. Out.
Nothing.
Up, down. Rise, fall. In, out.
Incredibly, her pulse slowed. Amazingly, she relaxed.
Mommy and Daddy will be home soon now, she thought.

Beneath her bed, nothing moved. Nothing breathed. Nothing clawed at the bedposts or tore at the edge of the quilt. Nothing smelled rotten. Nothing whispered in the dust.

She started to hum. At first it came out dry; she had no spit in her throat and her voice box didn't work. Then she swallowed twice and tried again.

The sound entered the room and everything was fine. The shadows receded. They lost depth and texture, fell back, faded out to make way for moonlight. The closeness of the room rose up above her head and dissipated. She extended her hands and feet again, feeling the edges of the mattress.

Rachel put words to the tune.

"Hush little baby, don't say a word. Mama's gonna buy you a mockingbird."

The high sweetness of her voice coursed warmth through her blood.

"And if that mockingbird don't sing—"

She stopped. Her breath caught in her throat.

"*Mama's gonna buy you a diamond ring*," the croaking voice beneath her bed finished.

In Rachel's nightmares, the worst moment always came when she reacted with a scream to whatever horrible thing happened, but no sound came out.

She tried to scream now, but no sound came out. Over and over. Again and again, until she tasted bile in the back of her throat. She didn't move. She didn't get out of bed. She didn't go rushing from the room. She was frozen. She was frozen, and something under her bed was perfectly willing to lie there and sing with her, sing her to death, scare her heart to splinters.

She was caught.

If Grandpa were here he'd take care of it, she thought desperately. *He always does. All he'd have to do is stare it down, and it'd go away.*

The thing under the bed growled softly.

He'd take care of it, Rachel thought, and despair shook her. Everything dark—above, below, inside, out.

The gloom was strong again. Something black, a shadow within a shadow, moved up the edge of the wooden bed frame with a rasping of claws.

Rachel saw it, heard it. She lay rooted, the pale skin of her ankle just inches from its scrabbling want. She felt her heart palpitate. The weight of the room's walls pressed down. With a whisper of breath she closed her eyes tight …

And then in a brilliant, shining instant, shifting light burned bright through the window blinds. Outside an engine purred, then stopped. Car doors opened and slammed shut. Boots crunched on snow. Daddy spoke quiet words. Mommy and Grandma responded.

The front door opened, and Rachel was free.

With a shriek she tore off her blankets and jumped out of bed. She sprinted across the bedroom and down the hall—straight into Daddy's arms.

"Whoa, now! What's this?" He hugged her tight, a flashlight in one hand.

She threw her arms around his neck, sobbing.

"Hey, hold on." Daddy held her at arm's length, smiling. "What's the matter? It's just a power outage."

"There's a monster under my bed!"

Daddy smiled. "Oh yeah? Let's go take a look together, huh? See how he holds up under my flashlight."

"*No*, Daddy, it's—"

"Come on, now."

They went back to the bedroom. They looked under the bed with the flashlight.

Nothing was there but dust and dirty socks.

Ten minutes later Rachel finally felt tired for the first time in hours. Tucked in tight, Daddy sitting on the edge of the bed reading *Mike Mulligan and His Steam Shovel* out loud, the flashlight's beam reassuring as it spilled off the pages of the book and onto the blankets, her eyes grew heavy.

Daddy looked tired, too. She could see it in his face. Everyone would sleep well. She didn't need light. All she needed was to know they were sleeping nearby, in the rooms around her.

"Mommy," she murmured. "Grandma. Can they come say goodnight?"

Daddy stopped reading and looked at her. "Mommy's ... Mommy and Grandma are real tired, Honey," he said.

"But it'll only take a minute."

"They're real sad now, Rachel. It—"

He stopped.

Rachel sat up straight—so straight she knocked the flashlight from Daddy's hand by mistake. It flipped backward and fell to the floor. The light went out. The sound of batteries rolling across the polished planks seemed to die before it could properly be heard.

"Why are they sad?" Rachel demanded.

In the dark, Daddy fumbled for the batteries. She could hear him. There, he had one ... There now, the other.

"Honey, in the morning. We'll talk more in the morning."

"Is Grandpa OK?" she asked, her voice very small.

Daddy said nothing. In the dark, all Rachel could hear was the sound of his hands fumbling with the pieces of flashlight and the batteries that made it work.

Then she heard something else.

"Daddy, turn the light on," Rachel breathed.

"Just give me a minute here," said Daddy, but his voice sounded odd, strange. It sounded upset in a way she'd never heard before.

"*Please*, Daddy. Hurry!"

"Hold your horses, now, I'm getting there."

"Daddy!"

Something black and hulking, a shadow within a shadow, stepped out from the corner of the room behind Daddy. It turned toward her. Two great tendrils of gloom reached forward.

"Almost got it, Honey. Almost."

"Too late," whispered Rachel, and shut her eyes tight.

Two Calls

Of course it was never as fine as his dreams, but still it was fine. The waves rolled on toward the shore. The world tilted on the edge of sight far out to sea. The sun slipped past its zenith and raced to fall, a comet across the water. Warm, bronzed people lay on the white sand, some already packing up, leaving for gritty showers at home, bare feet kicking up powder. A few, final Venice Beach street merchants plied their trades in the fading light—incense sticks, charcoal portraits, power crystals and sea-shell animals. Half a block down, a guitarist, case open for change, played a sad song about something lost forever.

Jacob stood, dusted off his swim trunks, and turned to his best friend.

"Dinner?"

"Sure," said Richard. "I should call Julie first. See how she's feeling."

"No problem. Call away."

Richard did. Frowning at his phone, he punched in the number to his home in Baltimore. His eyes took on a far-away look, glazed and sightless, and Jacob knew he could no longer see the great halo of light that glowed like a path from the shore to the rolling Pacific horizon. He saw other things instead.

Then Richard began talking, phone to one ear, a finger in the other, turning off the far-away guitar and the hum of the waves, the sea gulls and the street vendors.

What, Jacob thought, are they saying to one another? He imagined a laundry list of things that needed to be done upon Richard's return: messages from work, small crises and tiny triumphs. The latest doctor report. Did the baby kick? Has it turned? Can Julie *feel* it?

Jacob walked toward the shore and sat down just above the tide line. He remembered his first vacation here, ten years before. He'd stopped the Venice Beach Hotel manager with a gentle tug of his sleeve and asked, "Do you ever get tired of this?"

"Of what?" the harried old man had asked.

"The beach. The people. Venice." He'd made a sweeping gesture with his arm.

And suddenly the old man's tired face had brightened. "Never," he said. "Look around."

Walking away, the manager had turned back. "Never!" he'd repeated.

Richard walked close and flopped down beside him. Jacob started to say something, then noticed he was still on the phone.

"If we go on Tuesday, that will give me two hours' extra time at work. Four days should be enough to find a decent rental. Yeah, OK. Fly out Tuesday, come back Saturday. Go ahead and book it for the end of the month. And don't let her get to you, Julie. You don't need the stress."

Jacob said nothing. He sat like a statue on the sand. Finally Richard tapped a button on his phone, folded it up, and put it in his pocket.

"Sorry about that," he said.

"No problem."

"There's lots going on at home right now, what with Julie's job and the baby coming soon. Insurance issues."

"That's fine. It's the same for me back in Pittsburgh... Hey, maybe we could wait on dinner for a bit. Let's walk over to those rocks. To the tidal pools. We could find a few more shells to bring home to our wives."

Richard snorted. "Already got eight jars full. Julie says she can't find anyplace else to put them! I'll give you whatever I've got back at the hotel and you can give them to Susan."

Jacob paused, blinked, then said, "Let's just walk awhile, then."

"Been walking all day."

"Just to the rocks."

"Fine, but my feet hurt."

They walked over to the rocks where the waves broke and climbed up on one, sheltered above the spray. Hermit crabs, starfish, mussels and minnows weaved in the ebb and flow of the pools beneath them. Three twelve-year-olds clambered up beside them, headed for a taller boulder. Years had passed since Jacob had climbed up that far: too much risk of a fall, of breaking something, and what was the point, anyway?

"Hell," he said, and followed the kids. At the top he stood next to them for a long moment, looking out to sea. A moment later he picked his way down again.

"Dinner?" he asked.

"About time," said Richard.

* * * * *

They sat down at an outdoor table at the Sidewalk Café. For ten years it had been a mutual favorite—ever since they started taking their annual "buddy trip" following high school graduation. Through a long decade the restaurant had never looked any different from one year to the next.

"Remember," said Jacob, "when you tripped over that dead seal on the beach in the dark one morning? Your foot sank right in!"

"Look, man, I'm about to eat, OK?"

Jacob tried again. "Or the second time we came here, right off the plane, and I had five glasses of Merlot, I was so happy to be away from college? Right at that table over there."

Richard smiled. "Me and Patrick and Kevin had to carry you back to the hotel."

Jacob nodded. "But only after three hours wandering around Santa Monica. The Third Street Promenade. Hey, you remember that Costa Rican girl, how she gyrated those hips? I spent fifteen bucks on that band's album, just so I could give her the money and see her smile at me."

"Did she smile?"

"Nope!" Jacob chuckled.

"She *was* gorgeous," Richard agreed.

"Hey, why didn't we go there this time? To the Promenade?"

"Jesus, I guess I forgot all about it."

"Me too."

"We've seen it all anyway."

A one-armed waiter took their order. Jacob looked toward the ocean. The sun was falling into it so fast he could see it moving.

"Good view from here," he said.

"View of what?" said Richard. He was flipping through his wallet and looking at receipts. "Some of these dinners are tax-deductible," he murmured.

"Never mind," said Jacob.

"Hey, what time does our flight leave tomorrow?"

"Noon."

"Too bad. I'll miss sleeping in."

"One more chance to walk Venice Pier and go to the Cow's End for breakfast if we get up early enough."

"I doubt that'll happen. Long flight, long drive after that. I need my sleep."

Dinner arrived, they ate, and the plates were taken away. Dessert and decaf coffee followed.

Richard looked at Jacob for a long moment. "It was a good vacation," he said, voice suddenly bright.

"Yes," said Jacob. "I hate to leave."

"It'll all still be here. It's not going anywhere."

"That's true," said Jacob. "You're right."

The last sliver of sun slipped beneath the distant waves. Red and gold light disappeared in an instant, leaving the terrace in blue darkness. The waiter with one arm came around to each table with lit candles.

"Hey," said Richard, that artificial brightness still in his voice, "I think you're right. We should eat at the Cow's End tomorrow morning."

"I'd like that."

"And what about the Promenade tonight?"

"I think—"

Richard's phone rang. "It's Julie again," he said. "I'll be right back." He got up and left the restaurant.

Jacob paid the bill. Then he, too, got up and left. He walked past the candlelit tables, passed Richard's voice talking distantly to a distant place, and into the darkness of the now-empty beach. He took a deep breath. Sea air filled his lungs. He listened carefully. Seagulls cried over the crash of waves. Behind him, all over Venice Beach, streetlights blinked on. Further down the boardwalk a group of teenagers laughed, a cloud of cigarette smoke billowing back in their wake.

He pulled out his cell phone. He dialed a number.

After three rings, someone picked up on the other end two thousand miles away.

"Hello, Susan?" he said. "Yes. Oh, I miss you too. Like you wouldn't believe. No, not since we talked this morning. Me too. Sure. We get in at eight. How's the baby?"

The Hunt

Biting wind whipped among the trunks of black trees, and branches, snow-laden, cracked to fall about the two young men as they pulled on hand-rolled cigarettes, loaded rifles under their arms. The slivers of sky they could see above the brittle canopy were deep gray. Moonlight reflected off clouds and spread bleak, shifting illumination across the land. Snow—incessant, pervasive—collected on the brims of their hats and in the cuffs of their trousers.

"Whittaker's field is only an easy half-mile off," said Samuel Holt, flicking the stub of his cigarette away. They watched as it tumbled through the air and came to rest hissing in the ice-crisped pine needles. The orange glow of the tip burned low, then out.

"Easy? Damned if that'll be an easy walk," said Arthur Hughes.

Samuel struck a match, and for a brief moment they stared at one another's pale, wide-eyed faces in the spluttering, abused light. A violent spat of wind plucked the match from his fingertips and blew out the flame in midair.

"Arthur, I swear you've seen a haunt. If you could see yourself like I see you, I doubt you'd argue the point."

"I don't need a ghost to scare me more. I guess this about caps it."

The woods ran up a gentle hill over Still Creek, then on, wilderness, for over thirty miles. People got lost and died in such woods. Arthur knew they were still within three miles of town, but in the dark and the cold and the snow, he wished they were out in Whittaker's field now, not a half-mile slog from it.

"Your father going to meet us by the oak?" Samuel asked, raising his voice above the crying wind.

"Said he would. Listen to that howl. It's getting bad again."

Samuel, always the better ear for such things, socked his arm. "Wait."

They listened.

"The wind…"

"No, not the wind," Samuel muttered. "Not the wind."

Arthur cursed and fumbled for the mining lantern at his side, touched the butt of his smoke to the wick, and shut the trap. A dull, faint glow took hold of the tallow and pushed back the night around them. In the distance, gunshots, then screams, superseded the howls that were not wind.

"They're flushing our way!" Samuel hissed.

"Should we make for Whittaker's field? I don't know if Pop'll still be there if—"

"That'd be moving away from them. We don't want to move away from them."

Arthur tugged the glove off his right hand with his teeth and stuffed it into a woolen coat pocket. The cold, naked flesh of his hand and fingers found fast reassurance around the colder wood of his rifle, and he grasped it until his knuckles went bloodless.

The cacophony grew clearer. Soon Arthur could make out faint lights coming down the hill. "They veering off?" he asked, pointing.

Samuel nodded. "*Now* we make for Whittaker's. They're driving them out into the open."

They ran until Arthur thought his lungs would bleed. He was a fine runner and he knew it, but the cold, the snow, the hill, the trees, the bushes and rocks all fought to take his air, fight his legs, slow him down, trip him up, and by the time the pale field opened up before them, the baying and the howling and the shouts and lanterns now very close and growing closer, he was just about spent.

Yet there was more to do.

"Jesus wept," gasped Samuel.

Arthur raised his eyes in time to see the first wolf, dark against the plane of snow, dart in for Mr. Rowling's hound, flip it over, and rip its throat out in a single, fluid motion. Rowling cursed and fired, and the wolf fell even as the hound let out half a wet yelp and went still. All around the field now the lights of lanterns stood out like candles, enveloping Whittaker's field in a spluttering, shifting glow.

The wolf pack, half-starved, driven to desperation by the worst winter in a century, turned to take its stand.

Ten hours before, in the kitchen back home, Arthur's father had said, "Only once in a blue moon. All other times they keep to themselves, give or take a sheep. God willing, you won't see this a second time, even if you live to be an old, old man. The days of wolves killing men will be over after tonight."

Yet here, now, was that one time, the night not yet over, and Arthur felt the pulse of fear beat hard in his temples and wrists.

"Spread out, boys! Don't want no crossfire. Aim low!" Old Victor Eugene, who had somehow trawled his way through the hunt with his bad leg and weak heart, bellowed, demanded attention, and got it. The pinpricks moved apart.

Arthur couldn't count the flitting shadows. The hounds put up a frantic clamor, taut bodies pulling tight against their tethers, squirming and raging, jumping up in front of the lanterns. The men shivered, bodies moved by wind, adrenaline, and other, darker things. The wolves moved on the periphery of his vision, pacing out of the night and back again. The hip lanterns were erratic, disorienting sources of illumination. He felt caught in a nightmare; nothing seemed real.

"A baker's dozen," Samuel muttered.

"How can you tell?" Arthur had time to ask, and then the wolves came on.

Later, no one argued that the hunting party was surprised by the sheer vivacity of the wolves during the final attack. The hunt was nine hours old, and for seven the hunters had closely pursued the starving pack with dog and gun. The wolves were exhausted, beleaguered, and dying.

Yet when they charged, some of the men hardly had time to loose their hounds and raise their rifles. Suddenly the darting forms were no longer on the edge of Arthur's sight, but far too close and clear.

They came against the hounds first. For a moment the party could only watch. The animals grunted as they slammed against one other, and for a half-breath of time the wolves fell at bay.

But the hounds were outnumbered, and some of the wolves, used to fighting, and desperate, struggled with a vigor that left dogs dead in their paths, regained their bearings, and continued the charge.

"Get 'em up! Aim! Fire!" someone shouted, and then the pinpricks of light disappeared as rifles exploded like canons across the field. Arthur blinked, eyes dazzled, and raised one hand from his rifle to his right temple.

"Look out! Arthur!"

Opening his eyes, Arthur saw the muzzle of Samuel's rifle flash. The percussion stunned his ears. A wolf, just spitting distance off, shrieked and began to limp away, then turned, disoriented, and plodded slowly toward Samuel again. It did not growl, but its teeth shone bright in a wide, uneven grin, even as Samuel took careful aim and fired a second time.

Only then did Arthur hear a faster padding on the snow, and smell, through the fumes of powder sulfur and lantern oil, a deep, wild musk.

He turned. Fear clenched his bowels like a vise.

And then he was screaming and screaming, and suddenly the screams were no longer of fear but of fury, and everything, dream-like before, became very real. His teeth clacked together in a tight grimace. His hands grasped the rifle in a clenched lock, and when the emaciated wolf leapt at him, hackles raised, dark eyes reflecting deep pools in the spluttering glow of his lantern, Arthur shot from the hip. One of the wolf's great eyes went darker but lost its depth.

A gout of blood exploded out the back of its head and darkened the snow. Its body somersaulted backward, legs and neck already rag-doll limp, and came to rest curled in an untrodden patch of field. The snow darkened around it.

Still screaming, he saw four-legged motion in the distance, ran forward, and fired again. And again. And once more.

When, finally, he heard only the clicks of the empty chambers, he flipped the rifle around and caught it by the barrels, ready to club whatever came on. Panting, rasping like a saw in the bitter air, Arthur looked about him wide-eyed, teeth reflecting moonlight.

Nothing else came on. For a moment Arthur was all alone, more alone than he had ever been.

Samuel started whistling behind him.

Arthur turned. On first sight Samuel seemed calm, but there was a shake to the tune that came from more than cold, and when he walked forward his gait was jerky, stilted and unnatural.

"Got a cigarette?"

"Here." Arthur dropped the rifle and fished in a coat pocket.

Samuel cupped his hand across the match Arthur offered him, pulled smoke deep into his lungs, and exhaled a fine, blue cloud from his mouth and nostrils.

A deep silence fell across Whittaker's field. To Arthur, the people moving across it seemed somehow diminished. The field itself seemed somehow smaller. The night seemed less dark. The moon seemed less bright.

Without talking, men moved among the dark, still swellings on the ground, kicking or poking each one. Several of the forms whimpered. Rifle muzzles belched flame. The smell of scorched fur mingled with sulfur on the wind.

When Arthur and Samuel found Arthur's father he was sitting on a rock underneath the big oak tree Whittaker never had the heart to cut down.

"You boys sound?" he asked.

"Fine, Mr. Hughes," said Samuel.

He looked to Arthur. "You?"

"Fine," said Arthur.

Mr. Hughes pulled out a plug of tobacco and bit off a piece. He chewed thoughtfully for a moment, then said, "You boys did good. I saw you. You did good."

He stood up and drew them toward him, put his hands on their shoulders, and shook them with gentle but firm earnestness. Arthur could never describe the expression he saw on his father's face at that moment, but he never forgot it.

Mr. Hughes then stepped back and sat down heavily on the rock again.

"They got old Eugene."

"What?"

Mr. Hughes turned and spit at the tree. "Victor Eugene's dead. Took a bad bite on the shoulder, but Moss Freeman saw the whole thing and thinks it was one part that, two parts heart attack."

"He shouldnt've been there," said Samuel. "Someone should've made sure he stayed home. He was too old."

Mr. Hughes laughed, face grim. "You ever get old Eugene to do anything he didn't wanna do? If so, you'd make a damn fine lawyer, but I have my doubts you did."

"Where's Dip? Where's the dog?" Arthur asked.

"Had to shoot him … I should have let him stay with you. Foolish of me. You needed him more."

"No," said Arthur, voice very soft, "No, I didn't."

Mr. Hughes looked up quickly. He nodded.

Arthur took a last, long pull at the stub of his cigarette, then turned and spit it from his mouth. He ached with exhaustion.

"Can we go home now? My feet are about frozen through."

"Yeah. Yeah, go on home. But don't mention Eugene. No one else need know about that until we've a chance to talk with his wife first, let her know what happened."

As they walked away, Arthur could feel his father's eyes on his back. When he turned, his father was already walking back across the field to where a group of very quiet men stood in a half-circle around a still form covered by a coat already dusted with snow.

Samuel walked beside Arthur and neither of them spoke for a long time. Arthur's lungs felt like half-frozen balloons. His right shoulder ached from the kickback of the rifle. The balls of his knees throbbed and the joints cracked every time he took a step.

They found the trail at the edge of the forest and soon smelled the wood smoke of chimney fires just as the stench of sulfur began to fade. As the trees thinned, Arthur saw distant lights coming from the windows of homes that promised hot soup and warm beds.

"This will never happen again," he said to Samuel, who was huffing along beside him.

"That's what your father said."

"You don't believe him?"

They stopped at the edge of the forest atop a hill overlooking the back yards of the houses on Main Street. The yards and the houses looked small to Arthur. Still Creek seemed far removed even though it was close. He didn't feel well.

"I do, but it's the damndest thing," said Samuel. "They're all dead but I don't feel safe. I wanna look back over my shoulder."

"This will never happen again," Arthur repeated. "They're all dead. Father said so. We won't see wolves here again. In the spring they'll make sure, take the dogs and root out any breeding dens. Any dens at all."

Some of the pain went out of Arthur's lungs as they stood still.

"I'm gonna sleep well tonight," Samuel said. "Glad tomorrow's Sunday and no work. Come over for lunch at noon. Mother's making mincemeat pie."

They parted ways as they came down the hill.

Arthur let himself into the house and went to his mother's warm embrace, hot cider, potato soup, and bread by the fire. He answered questions as shortly as possible. He kept thinking about what Samuel had said—about wanting to look over his shoulder. He was very tired and wanted to sleep, so he ate quickly then went to his room. The room seemed smaller.

Later, lying in bed and looking up at the slanted beams of the roof that met over his head, Arthur heard the back door close and his father's voice and footsteps. His parents spoke in hushed tones for a long while. For a time he heard his mother crying, but eventually those noises ceased. Finally, like always, the whole house fell silent.

I'm so tired, he thought all the rest of the long night.

Lorna Gould's Roses

Glenda Hall offered me another cup of tea, but I politely declined. Its aftertaste, mingled with the aftertaste of her muffins, was faintly appalling.

"It's good of you to visit, Henry," she said, setting down the pot. "Your grandmother always spoke so highly of you. You eat up and I'll give you the photographs you're after."

"That would be great, Mrs. Hall," I said, leaving the muffins alone and checking my watch. "I *am* a bit pressed for time."

The old lady clucked her tongue. "The young are always in a hurry, but there's something to be said for taking the time to smell the roses."

My eyes traveled to a glass vase standing next to the plate of muffins on the coffee table. It was full of red tea roses, freshly cut.

"You like them?" she asked.

"Very nice. From your own garden?"

"Oh, heavens no. I could never grow roses like that. Those are from next *door*. You saw the burnt house?"

"Yes. I meant to ask you about that."

"A shame, that is. Terrible. But the garden is still as good as when Lorna Gould planted it fifty-seven years ago. She had quite the green thumb." A far-away look came into her eyes. Macular degeneration had left them half-blind, but from the outside looking in, they seemed quite clear.

"What happened?" I asked.

"Hmm? To Lorna Gould? She died four years ago, age of ninety-two. I got her beat." Mrs. Hall winked.

"No, I meant what happened to the house?"

"Oh, that! *There's* a story for you. Got five minutes?"

I hesitated, then nodded.

"Well," she said, leaning in and setting a bony, confidential hand on my leg, "Lorna always kept her house nice. Took pride in it. You used to visit me with your grandmother when you were little, so you might remember."

I nodded, trying not to betray my distaste. Glenda Hall had never liked children, and I hadn't exactly changed her mind about them all those years ago, if memory served. But she and Grandma had belonged to the same bridge club, and Grandma had enjoyed showing me off to her friends.

"Nicest house on the block," Mrs. Hall continued. "Always a pleasure to have Lorna as a neighbor. Her husband was the last mine foreman in Still Creek, you know. It takes a special kind of woman to marry a man like that. Had to have an iron will to match his, and she did. But even strong wills bend with age, and when she died, she hardly knew her own name. According to some, her death, under such circumstances, was passingly sad but long overdue. I visited her just before she went, and for what it's worth, I tend to agree."

I nodded, forcing myself to bite into one of the muffins. Echoes of bad childhood memories came flooding back with the stale taste.

"Well, once that house went up on the market, I knew there'd be trouble. And of course there was. It wasn't two weeks before the Danforths moved in, and right away things started going downhill."

"How's that?"

Mrs. Hall whistled. "First off, they had five cats. *Five cats!* You ever hear of such a thing? And a tall, mangy mutt to boot. Big and lanky, like a German Shepherd but not pure. Kept it chained up in the back yard beside an old wooden house made of particle board. I thought it would wear a hole into the ground from all that pacing. And the barking! Night and day. Day and night. It was enough to send an old lady's nerves over the edge, let me tell you!"

"I can imagine."

"Well, the wife was fat and wore dirty shirts that said dirty things. And the husband swore enough to turn the grass black. And their *children*? Little urchins! Always screaming and crying and rolling in the dirt. The lawn was the first to go. Lorna's lovely lawn. And those children *rolled* in the remains!"

"Imagine that."

"Yes! Imagine that! And then Mr. Danforth, he started parking his old rusted pickup on the *front lawn*, and he dragged a davenport out on the *front porch*. Five months. *Five months*, and that was all it took to undo Lorna's lifetime of work on that nice old house."

"Hard to believe."

"Yes! Hard to believe! Here, eat that muffin, now."

My stomach churned. "Oh no—two filled me up fine."

"Nonsense!"

"No, really, I'm fine, Mrs. Hall."

For a moment I thought Mrs. Hall would say something more, but she didn't press any further.

"Well, anyway, pretty soon Mr. Danforth got to hitting Mrs. Danforth, and she always had dark glasses on to hide her black eyes, and then *she* starting hitting the *children*, and after that some of the cats even began to limp a bit. During Parade Day Mr. Danforth got in a great big fight right in the middle of the street with some other fellow, and that was ugly for everyone. Oh, and one time Mrs. Danforth threw a vase through the bedroom window. Things like that give Still Creek a bad name, you know."

I nodded.

"And the ladies up at the Bridge Lodge started talking about it, because really it was all getting to be a bit much. And then, one day, I heard Mrs. Danforth yelling at Mr. Danforth to—" she gulped, "to *dig up those goddamn roses*, pardon my language. Can you imagine the *nerve?* And I knew that just wouldn't do. Really, it wouldn't."

I shook my head in mock regret, glancing down at my watch.

"But things have a way of taking care of themselves," she continued, placing that confidential hand on my leg again. "At least, that's what my Samuel always used to say before he passed away, God rest him. And sure enough, late that very same night, when the Danforths were out at some drag racing contest by the fairgrounds, the house caught fire and burned right down to the basement foundation. Let me tell you, it lit up the night like the Fourth of July! A bunch of cats and that dog of theirs died, and all their junk burned up, too. Even that old davenport on the front porch!"

Her hand had closed on my leg like a talon. I winced but pretended not to notice. "Did ... did they ever find out what caused it?" I asked.

"Oh, arson they think."

"Any arrests?"

"Nope! The police talked to lots of people, of course. But they didn't arrest anyone. Anyone at all."

I glanced up. Mrs. Hall was smiling, and that far-away look was back in her half-blind eyes. Again, to me they looked surprisingly clear, and when she caught my gaze she gave me a wink.

"I... I suppose Mrs. Gould would have been pleased," I said lamely.

"Oh, Lorna hated her roses being bothered. She never gave a single one away through all her years. Not ever. Not a single one to anyone...and finally I knew that just wouldn't do. Really, it wouldn't."

Suddenly she snapped to. "You *sure* you won't have another bite of that muffin? I have to say, in my experience most people only eat like a bird when they don't like the food! I baked them myself, you know. And I *hate* to see a grown man go hungry."

No, I thought quickly. *That just wouldn't do.*

Without a word, I picked up a muffin and took a big bite. Then another. I smiled, chewed, and swallowed. Again and again.

"More tea?"

I nodded.

"There, now, *that's* better!" Mrs. Hall said, pouring out another cup and giving me a sunny smile. "I'll go find those photographs."

She bustled out of the room. I looked down at the plate of muffins next to the vase of red tea roses from Mrs. Gould's garden, freshly cut. There were six muffins left on the plate. Lifting my teacup to my lips, I vowed to eat them all.

Birthday

He could trace his motivation back to a single memory. All the years of work and toil; of diligent research and public ridicule; of failure, despair, more failure, and, finally, after half a *century*—

Success.

Seventy-six years old to the day, hair white, skin pale, eyes rheumy, David Halburn sat back in his swivel chair and looked at what stood before him.

A time machine.

"Thomas Wolfe, eat your heart out," he murmured through dry lips. "I'm going home again."

* * * * *

"Mommy, what's that man looking at?"

David's sixth birthday party breathed magic. Outside, the world grew green and smelled of warm earth, flowers, and bees. Sunshine fell through white curtains, heating the yellow carpet, illuminating chubby faces of kindergarten friends. His house, huge in mystery and secure in safety, blazed with banners, streamers, balloons and confetti. In the center of the living room, a great birthday cake with "E.T." carefully drawn on the top in icing awaited inevitable destruction. Chocolate ice cream sat cooling in the freezer. Wrapped presents, bulky in ways that promised Transformers and GI Joes,

Star Wars figures and He-Men, rose up on the coffee table like an offering, a celebration, a reward for being born.

In the hallway, children played "Pin The Tail on the Donkey." In the den, an ATARI 2600 blipped to the tunes of "Pitfall" and "Tron." In the living room, his father, quick to laugh and easy with life, detached his thumb with causal aplomb, then wiggled it to applause. And sitting on a chair while his mother tied his shoe, David stared through the open bay window and wondered aloud about the strange man in the street.

His mother, still girlish in early womanhood, looked where he was pointing and smiled. "It's just an old man," she said. "He's probably thinking about all the fun we're having in here."

The old man stood in the street, staring at the house, an odd expression on his face. David looked again. Their eyes met.

"He looks sad," he said.

"Maybe he's remembering what it was like to be young like you," his mother said, turning back to the offending shoelace. "Maybe he doesn't have anybody, and seeing your party makes him think back on happier times."

"Will I ever be old like that?" David asked.

His mother leaned forward and kissed his cheek.

"Not for a very, very long time," she said. But that wasn't the same as "never," and David knew it.

Then the call came to light the candles on the cake, and for a long, long time—many years—his sorrow was forgotten.

* * * * *

But time, whatever else one may say about it, is dependably punctual. Years passed as surely as clockwork, taking with them seasons, family, friends, and any feelings of security he had once possessed. True, it gave as well as took; wisdom, perspective, knowledge, maturity, and love all found their way into his life when he wasn't looking, and all were welcomed. Yet loss, that feeling of watching sand run through your fingers all the faster as you try to stop it, became first a dim background distraction, then an annoyance… and then, finally, an obsession.

Favorite places changed. Favorite people grew old and passed away. Summer faded against a background of work in windowless rooms. Winter, no longer a wonderland, became a battleground for deep-freeze wars with cracked carburetors and icy roads.

And then…

Then…

David's father called his apartment, voice quavering, heavy with the news that his mother was riddled with cancer.

"This isn't supposed to happen," David told her as she lay in her hospital bed and tried to smile. "You're not supposed to die."

"Funny, I thought the same thing!" she said softly. Her laughter became a long series of wracking coughs before trailing off.

"Grandma Rose and Grandpa Ted, Aunt Emily and Uncle James. My rabbit, Flopsy. My dog. Two dozen pets and half a dozen relatives. Five friends. All of them gone, each loss a chip with a chisel, a tap with a hammer. I'm being worn down by death, Mom. And you—"

"Me," she repeated.

"A great sledgehammer blow that will shatter me to pieces." Tears rolled freely down his cheeks.

"David."

He shook his head.

"David, look at me."

He raises his red eyes, and only then did he remember that long-ago birthday party so deeply buried beneath other memories.

"This is the way of the world," said his mother, her voice drifting up into the room from a far-away place. "It's natural. A mother isn't supposed to outlive her son. Time rolls around and the great game continues, but with other players, each possessing a part of those who came before. You live in me, I live in you."

"It's damned unfair, Mom," he said. "Everyone says it's the way of things. I don't care. It doesn't make the loss any easier."

"You don't have a choice," she murmured, strength fading away. "*That* makes it easier."

We'll see, he thought, even as he nodded and tried to smile. *We'll see*.

* * * * *

The time machine wasn't, of course, a constant project. He tinkered with it now and then, here and there, but always it was in the back of his mind, a comfort, tantalizing, a bright spot to stave off despair. He married, had children of his own, watched them grow. He didn't worry as his hair turned gray, didn't pine away as his little girl married, didn't flinch in the face of clocks.

Once it's done, I can see it all again whenever I want. The thought sustained him through long years and short, bad years and good.

Unlike Jay Gatsby, he had no illusions about repeating the past. Childhood was gone. The years behind were more numerous than the years ahead. But to be able to chat with his grandfather, pet his old dog, see his children young again, watch his mother laugh—*that* was the great desire, the burning hope. He was fervently convinced that loss was responsible for old age, more than anything else. To skip back and forth, skimming the surface of time like a rock across a still, clear pool—it would be a retirement gift fit for the gods, a chance at peace such as he had not known in a long, long time.

Now, a palsied hand caressed the cool metal skin of the device, finally finished. Gently, two brittle legs stepped into the machine's small chamber.

David closed his eyes, smelling the oiled gears, taking stock of a million choices.

After long moments, silent save for the tick of his watch, he brushed his hands across a series of buttons, pulled a lever, twisted a dial, and, eyes still closed, held on tight.

* * * * *

1994, he thought, looking out. *A good year*.

More than anything, he wanted to see his mother. She wouldn't recognize him, of course, and he wouldn't say anything to even remotely suggest who he was.

On his sixteenth birthday the teenaged David had been in Florida visiting friends over Spring Break. His father would be at work. His mother?

Home.

He stepped out of the machine, which had materialized in an empty lot at the top of his old street.

A man with car trouble, that's who he was. Could he use the phone? And she would say yes, and he would be inside his childhood home again—once more part of the world he had left behind, if only for a moment. During that moment he would breathe in the ambiance of living memories, feel the near-silent hum of youth reborn.

He whistled as he walked down the street, past the old, familiar houses that would eventually be demolished to make way for a new bypass, past the trees that smelled, for one glorious week a year, of apple blossoms that carpeted the street and paved the sidewalk with delicate white petals.

I remember when they were cut up by the construction men and uprooted by the bulldozers, he thought.

He breathed in, smiled, exhaled, and continued on.

His house, when it came into view, shocked him. It was far, far smaller than he remembered. Yet it felt familiar, like an old pair of shoes not worn in years that still retained the contours of his feet. It felt familiar, and that meant comfort. It was *right*.

But what *wasn't* right were the cars in the driveway. And the E.T. balloons tied to the mailbox. And the children who laughed and played beyond the open front door.

No one is supposed to be here but Mom, he thought. *Not in 1994.*

He stopped, lost in thought.

Which means... which means...

This isn't 1994.

One inadvertent jerk of a finger, one wrong number. He should have paid closer attention.

Twenty feet away, his sixth birthday party was in full swing.

Just a quick glimpse, he thought, still planning on making that phone call. *Yes, a broken-down car, that'll do.*

His eyes, slightly glazed, focused again.

His mother sat framed in the great bay window, tying the shoe of a small boy he almost recognized.

"Mom!" he screamed, heart pounding. All thoughts of concealing his identity were instantly forgotten. There she was, young and healthy and smiling and full of life. "Mom, it's me!" he called out.

But all that issued up from his throat was a whisper.

I want my mother, he thought, and took a heavy step forward.

The child he almost recognized turned and caught sight of him.

"Mommy, what's that man looking at?"

His breath caught in his throat.

No, he thought numbly.

"He looks sad," the little boy said.

"Maybe he's remembering what it was like to be young like you," David's mother responded. "Maybe he doesn't have anybody, and seeing your party makes him think back on happier times."

"Will I ever be old like that?" little David asked.

His mother leaned forward and kissed his cheek.

"Not for a very, very long time," she said.

The offending shoelace now firmly tied and double-knotted, David and his mother rejoined the party. In the background, a dim shadow, his father placed candles on the cake, whistling cheerfully.

Outside, in a sunlight that didn't seem as warm or as bright as he had once remembered, David turned, smiling faintly, and walked slowly back up the street toward a time that was his own.

He missed it very much.

The Piano

A solid, cherry-stained Chickering, it has stood in Grandma's living room for seventy-two years. Her parents gave it to her in 1935, an early wedding present. Each key, starting with the first on the left, bears a tuner's date, and those run up until 1971. After that, nothing. Thirty-six years without a tune, and the river of people who touch the keys has slowed to a trickle, then run dry over slow but inexorable decades.

Apparently many played it back in the day, although I find that hard to believe. Ever since I can remember it has stood like any other piece of furniture: a silent prop—the bench a place for piles of newspapers and magazines, the flat top above the tuning wires a table for doilies, framed photos, and trinkets from Spain and France. I now sit by it, bumping a pile of *Newsweeks* that slide to the floor in a cascade.

"My fingers used to fly across the keys," Grandma tells me, rocking in her blue easy chair across the room. Only fifteen feet away, the piano is beyond her field of vision. "It's still a good piano, but it needs tuning, and I can't play it anymore."

"Did Mom used to play it?" I ask, stacking up the magazines.

"She sure did. She was very talented. All through high school she practiced on that piano. I don't know why she gave it up."

I nod, glancing around with mute contentment. The whole living room is a time capsule; a steady, warm element in a life full of change.

I am almost thirty, and all the other places from my childhood have gone away—or I have gone away from them.

Then I turn to Grandma again, and my contentment fades. She is ninety-four, and the last three years have not been kind.

"I have no idea who's going to take it," she says abruptly.

"Hmm? What's that?"

"Who's going to take it once I'm gone." She's looking toward the wooden cover over the keys.

"Oh, don't worry about that."

"No one I know would want it. Your uncle doesn't have room and your mother no longer plays. I don't think you'd want it, either. It's a shame."

"Oh, Grandma, I'd love to have it, but there isn't much room in my house."

"That's all right. I understand."

"I'm sure Mom would be thrilled with it. Besides, there's no reason to think about that right now. You're not going anywhere anytime soon."

But she doesn't look convinced. I think of her losses, which are too numerous to list. She knows better. I wonder, fleetingly, if there is *anything* left from her youth that hasn't yet gone away.

A little while later she goes out to the kitchen and makes supper for us—biscuits and chicken. The biscuits are burnt and the chicken too salty, but it's a good meal. I eat it all.

After we wash the dishes I say goodbye. She presses a check into my hand. Without looking, I know it's for fifty dollars. Without looking, I can picture her shaky script perfectly. I try to refuse it but she insists. Then I step out into the cool October afternoon and unlock the car.

When I was little, my grandparents always waved at me from the door as the family drove away. Now, as I drive off alone, it's just Grandma who sees me off. She watches until I'm down the road and long out of her sight. Through the rearview mirror I see her front door finally close.

Three blocks away, I realize I've forgotten a pot of russet mums she gave me for my front yard. It's still sitting on the walk beside the driveway. She'll be hurt if I don't go back for it. I turn the car around.

She doesn't hear my tires crunch the driveway stones. I pick up the flowers and pop the trunk.

And it's only then, holding the flowers in my hands, leaning over the car, that I hear it: faint but clear, the sound of the piano.

Through the closed front door I listen to my grandmother playing a song that is eighty-one years old. I know it because of a ninth grade history project I once completed on the "Roaring '20s." She knows it because it was a song of her youth.

She doesn't sing, but I know the words:

Blackbird, blackbird,
Singing the blues all day
Right outside of my door.
Blackbird, blackbird,
Why do you sit and say,
"There's no sunshine in store."
All through the winter you hung around.
Now I begin to feel homeward bound.
Blackbird, blackbird,
Gotta be on my way.
Where there's sunshine galore…

The piano hasn't been tuned in thirty-six years. Grandma has arthritis in her wrists and hands. She can hardly see, and misses keys.

I walk away before the song ends. It ushers me off, a living warmth from a long-gone time, an old thing that somehow hasn't aged.

That evening I call Grandma and tell her not to worry about the fate of the piano—when the time comes, I'll *make* room. And I'll be sure to play it.

"Well!" she says, surprised but pleased. "What made you change your mind?"

I make up an excuse. How can I possibly tell her that I heard her play—and that to me, every note sounded perfect?

Arachno

The night shift dragged on, and the two Rose Asylum attendants watched the camera feed from Cell 142 with all the interest they could hope to rouse. Most of the patients were asleep or restrained, either zonked out on hypodermic Quaaludes or strapped down to their beds. But the patient in Cell 142, Ms. Burgett, was wide awake. That meant amusement for Pete Younker and Mike Cavell.

Tonight, Cavell noted that Younker had again taken up one of his favorite entertainments. The knapsack he carried bulged in a familiar way, and when Dr. Peterson finally checked out for the night shortly after eleven, leaving them alone, Younker slipped out the jar.

"Not a bad catch," he told Younker, eyeing the fat, sluggish flies.

"Two weeks of night duty in a row, I figured we deserved a bit of fun," Younker replied. "Let's go."

They left the front office and unlocked the gate, passed through, then locked it tight again. They walked in the middle of the corridor so none of the patients in the barred cells could get in a good grab. Some of them knew how to gum out their meds and play 'possum at night, waiting for the right time to lash out a fumbling hand or tripping leg. And that, Cavell knew, was sometimes all it took. Walking the patient halls always made him nervous. He was a thin man, tall but not strong. Younker, on the other hand, was a massive slab of rough muscle, which came in handy at Rose Asylum. Cavell always appreciated his presence.

They stopped at Ms. Burgett's cell. It was secured by bulletproof glass, not bars. Cavell turned up the lights, and the cell went from dark to dim. Ms. Burgett hated light; anything stronger than a forty-watt bulb sent her into a frenzy. She was also allergic to most sedatives, so following Dr. Peterson's orders they did their best to accommodate her in small ways.

The room's contents—a bed, toilet, rounded plastic desk, and several badly mangled sketchbooks—gained definition.

"Where's her latest creation?" Cavell asked. "It was getting big."

"Dr. Peterson had Delaney take it out earlier this afternoon. Said it was getting too difficult to move around in there with all that yarn."

Cavell was always impressed by Ms. Burgett's sheer, inexhaustible creative drive when it came to yarn. Dr. Peterson only allowed yarn that would come apart easily—in case Ms. Burgett ever got an urge to hang herself. If she acted up, Dr. Peterson removed the yarn immediately, but good behavior resulted in several bolts, all gray like she liked. Ms. Burgett would then immediately set to it with her fingers and teeth, prodding, pulling, licking, winding, separating each strand and stretching it from bed spring to desk, toilet to shelf. The more yarn she was given, the more docile she became. Sometimes she spent whole days sitting in the middle of her creation, weaving more, until Dr. Peterson decided it had grown too big, too unhygienic, and had it cleaned out. Then Ms. Burgett, after the inevitable violent fit, would begin again when given another bolt.

"Can't see her," Younker grunted. "Under the bed again, I guess."

Cavell knew Ms. Burgett got cranky as hell when her cell was bare. She often took to hiding under her bed with the sulks. There was one sure-fire way to get her out, though, and Cavell knew what it was. He scratched lightly on the Plexiglas with a fingernail, and Younker held the jar of flies up to the tray slot.

Ms. Burgett moved like lightning. Still pressed flat to the floor, she scuttled out from under the bed, completely naked, and covered the ten feet to the flies in an instant, still on all fours. Then, with a sudden lunge, she slammed herself against the glass, clawing at it with three-inch fingernails, licking at it with her bright red tongue, biting at it with filed-sharp teeth. Clicking noises came from the back of her throat. They hardly sounded human.

Cavell recoiled. He would never grow used to Ms. Burgett's appearance, and certainly not to her mannerisms. He shuddered to think the woman had once been free.

"Down," said Younker.

Ms. Burgett immediately fell back in a splayed crouch. She scuttled sideways a few feet, never taking her wide eyes off the jar.

Satisfied, Younker unscrewed the lid and held the open mouth to the tray slot. The flies quickly filled the cell, and Ms. Burgett went to work. The clicking rose in pitch and frequency as she scampered around the chamber, still on all fours, ropes of drool running down her chin as she gnashed her teeth and, methodically, efficiently, caught her prey and dined.

Younker chuckled. "By God, our Black Widow's a little Renfield, isn't she?"

Cavell, stopwatch in hand, couldn't help but shiver as he smiled.

* * * * *

Like so many cases of criminal insanity, it was the smell that cost Ms. Burgett her freedom.

Cavell had seen her case file only once, and briefly at that, but had heard rumors in far greater detail: How the police had entered her apartment after neighbors reported the stench of rotting flesh emanating from beneath the door. How they had found three dogs, five cats, a dozen rabbits, and a seventy-five-year-old man wrapped up in fishing line, all hanging from the ceiling and quite dead. How Ms. Burgett had descended from a dense web of fishing line on a rope cord tied around her waist and attacked the officers with her sharpened teeth and nails. How her apartment was filled with a vast, moving carpet of tiny spiders, filling the cabinets, the washing machine, the toilets, the closets, and running rampant across the floors, walls and ceilings…

"Psychotic Monomania resulting in Schizophrenic Arachnophilia," was how Dr. Peterson offhandedly summarized Ms. Burgett's condition.

"Black Widow," was how the attendants described her.

After settling back into the office once they finished the rest of their rounds, Younker shook his head and whistled. "I finally got a good look at the Black Widow's fingers," he said.

Cavell had pulled out a report sheet and was starting to fill it out. A patient had vomited twice earlier that night, and Dr. Peterson and the morning nurses needed to be aware of it. "Hmm? What about them?"

"No prints," he replied. "I heard about that, but wanted to see for myself. They're smooth. Same with her feet and toes. Doctors think she sanded them off at some point, before she got caught."

"Jesus! Why?"

Younker shrugged and swung his feet up onto the desk, which creaked beneath the weight. "Why not? The chick's a loony. Anyway, that's why she's never been positively ID'd."

"I didn't know that."

"Sure. Peterson thinks she did it cause it was a way of 'further distancing herself from her human identity,' or something like that."

Cavell knew 'Ms. Burgett' wasn't the Black Widow's real name. She'd used it while in residence at the apartment building where she'd been caught, but beyond that the name had no apparent significance. The identification card the police recovered was false, and there were no credit cards, Blockbuster memberships, or telephone calls to provide further clues or leads. An intensive and extensive national records search had turned up nothing. If, like Dr. Peterson suggested, she had wanted to remove herself from the workings of human civilization, in that respect, if in no other, she had succeeded.

"Next time," Younker mused, "I think I'm gonna make her jump through a hoop for those flies."

"She won't listen," Cavell said, turning back to his report. "She doesn't play games for anyone."

"Even spiders can be trained." Younker yawned, flicked on the desk radio, and settled down for a quick nap.

* * * * *

"Hey, how long's it been since we last fed the Widow from the jar?"

For Cavell, time passed strangely in Rose Asylum. The redundancy and tedium of routine was largely to blame, but not entirely. The strangeness of the asylum's occupants: that played a part, too. News had no meaning inside. When he and Younker spoke of current events while on shift, the subjects seemed vague and distant. It was hard to speak of hockey games and presidential policy when people down the hall were screaming about bugs under their skin or how they intended to consume their parents. A day sometimes felt like a week, a week a month, a month a day.

"I don't know," Cavell replied. "Two weeks? Maybe less? I'm not sure."

Younker yawned. It was just after three in the morning. "Well, I thought we might have another go. I'm getting bored."

"Flies again?"

Younker smiled. "Nope. Check this out." He reached into his backpack and pulled out the familiar jar. But inside…

Cavell blinked. "*Fire*flies?"

"Easier to get this time of year."

Cavell wasn't sure how much fun fireflies would be. "It'll be over pretty quick," he said. "They'll probably just walk along the walls."

"Come on, let's go," Younker growled. "It's better than nothing."

This time, Ms. Burgett wasn't under her bed. Dr. Peterson had recently given her three bolts of yarn for good behavior, so she was now sitting secure in the middle of a great, connected mesh of damp fabric.

"Looky here, Black Widow," Younker said, waving the jar.

Ms. Burgett flexed, still in a crouch, then pounced against the window with a hiss.

Younker put the jar behind his back. He glanced at Cavell. "Let's see if we can make her dance a little."

Cavell looked at Younker uncertainly. "We shouldn't rile her up. You know she doesn't listen to anything but 'down.'"

"Oh, c'mon, it'll be fun." Younker returned his attention to Ms. Burgett. "Here now, spin a little for me." He twirled his finger in front of her face. "Spin round, little spider, spin round."

Ms. Burgett sneered at Younker, but kept an eye on the jar. She clicked and hissed and raked the glass with her nails, but Younker kept twirling his finger.

Cavell doubted she would listen even if she could understand… but then Ms. Burgett surprised him. Scowling, she suddenly crawled in a quick circle and hunkered down by the window, submissive but still clicking rapidly. Her eyes now never left Younker.

"There, you see? She learns fast." Younker flashed a grin at Ms. Burgett and unscrewed the lid of the jar. Carefully, he knocked the fireflies into the tray slot and stepped back to watch.

Ms. Burgett pounced. She took two immediately, one in each hand, slammed them into her mouth, and scurried back to the center of her nest. She chewed with gusto, grinning in a way that made Cavell want to lock himself back in the office, safe until the morning crew arrived.

"Look at that smile," said Younker. "She couldn't be happier."

Yes she could, Cavell thought. *From all accounts she seemed pretty damned happy in her old apartment, when the prey was bigger.*

And then, abruptly, Ms. Burgett stopped chewing. Her eyes became white saucers. Her lips, glowing dully with stains of fading luminescence, drew together in a tight, bloodless line.

"Younker?" Cavell stepped back.

Ms. Burgett took a long, deep breath.

Younker frowned. "Hey, what's her problem?"

The ensuing shriek was so loud Cavell and Younker called out and clapped their hands to their ears. Immediately the other patients, ripped from slumber, began to moan and cry.

"Now you've done it," Cavell said. "Come on."

But Younker was still staring at Ms. Burgett, entranced. Shrieking and hissing, she flailed at the glass, scrabbling at it in mad fury. She fell back, ripping at her tangled black hair. Blood spilled from her mouth; she had bitten into her tongue and lips with her filed teeth.

"Get the jar and let's go," Cavell said. "We have to let her calm down, and she won't with us here."

"Fine," said Younker. "Jesus, look at her."

"I already did. Let's go."

The shrieking ceased.

Cavell and Younker stepped carefully toward the cell, peering into the dim depths.

Gray yarn swayed in the aftermath of Ms. Burgett's frenzy. Through it they could see her crouched against the far wall. She was staring at them and smiling.

Cavell tapped Younker's sleeve with a shaking finger. "All right, she's calm now. Let's go."

"Yes, let's go."

Their footsteps echoed loud and rapid down the long corridor.

* * * * *

Cavell slammed a book down on the table.

"I figured out what went wrong yesterday," he said. "Fireflies. Listen here: 'Firefly bioluminescence is caused by a chemical reaction in the light organs. Predators avoid eating fireflies because these chemicals give off a bitter, musky taste, and can be toxic to amphibians, reptiles, arachnids, and other insects.' There you go. She thought you were trying to poison her...or at the very least didn't like the taste."

Younker picked up the book and looked at the spine. "*A Field Guide to North American Insects*. You just happen to have that lying around your house?"

"I like to read."

Younker chuckled. "Whatever. Good job, detective." He handed the book to Cavell and nodded toward a slip of blue paper pinned to the bulletin board. "I guess we'll find out tonight whether she bears a grudge. You see what's at the top of our duties?"

"I haven't even taken off my coat yet."

"Check it out."

Cavell squinted at Dr. Peterson's nearly indecipherable handwriting.

"Wait a minute."

Younker slapped Cavell on the back. "The Widow's nest has gotten too large again! And who gets to clean it out? Me and thee."

Cavell sighed. "I'd just as soon clean the latrines."

Younker grinned. "That's on the list too."

Ms. Burgett's web had grown impressively dense during the last few days. The floor, walls, and ceiling were covered with yarn. The bed and table could hardly be seen.

"The yarn…it looks almost *sticky*."

"It is," said Younker. "She licks every strand."

"I hate spiders," Cavell said, shivering slightly. "I don't mind them behind glass or on TV, but…anytime I see one I kill it if I can."

"Yeah? Try stepping on this one."

"Oh, shut up."

"We'll need to secure her arms," Younker said. "That's how the day shift usually does it."

Cavell turned up the light in the cell to forty watts. "I can't see her."

"Keep your stick handy, and your taser, too." Younker held up a pair of scissors. "I'll cut away a few of the bigger sections close to the door, you hang tight next to me, and then we'll see about getting her secure and finishing the rest of the cleanup. Ready?"

"No."

"Good enough for me." Younker typed in the lock code and the glass door slid quietly aside.

"It's humid in here. One of us should talk to Peterson about having the ventilation checked." Younker started snipping away. The skein of yarn began to slough off in great clumps he then kicked out into the passage.

"Do you see the Widow?"

"No. Ouch! Jesus!"

"What? *What?*" Cavell raised his stick.

"Put that damn thing down. Oh, man." Younker sucked on his thumb. "A goddamn spider bit me."

"Come again?"

"A spider! A spider, Cavell."

"Come here."

"Eh?"

Cavell stepped forward and pulled Younker into the light of the hallway. "There's two more on your shirt." He pointed to the tiny brown spiders but made no move to brush them away.

"The Widow's got her own little fan club in there, don't she?" Younker batted the spiders off with his stick. They drifted to the floor on gossamer threads, hit ground, and scurried back toward the cell. Younker was too quick. He brought his boot down hard. They sounded like bitten grapes as their abdomens burst.

Ms. Burgett moved quickly. Before Younker could turn she was on his back, shrieking as she slashed at his face with her claws.

Blast it, Younker, first the fireflies, now you kill her friends, Cavell thought, then brought the night stick down on Ms. Burgett's arm. There was a *crack*, louder than Younker's screams, and Ms. Burgett fell off his back. Cavell raised his stick again. Ms. Burgett lunged forward and caught it with her good hand. Younker, still screaming, fumbled for his taser, flicked it on, and jammed it into Ms. Burgett's neck. Blue lightning sizzled across her face, leapt across her filed teeth, and arced down her chest.

Younker pulled away.

Ms. Burgett fell.

Breathing hard, Younker and Cavell leaned heavily against the glass. Younker sobbed in distress, his face a criss-crossed pattern of welts and scratches. Cavell had his hand on his heart. It was pounding furiously.

"It…it shouldn't have done that," panted Younker. "The taser. She was damp. The current hit her too hard. She…check her pulse, Cavell."

Cavell inched forward as Younker slid down the glass and slumped to the floor, patting his bloody face with his shirtsleeve and moaning.

Ms. Burgett lay on her face. Her limbs looked wrong, somehow. Cavell reasoned the taser juice must have tightened them up. He grasped her unbroken arm to turn her over, but recoiled as he touched the skin. The arm felt funny, like the bones were in the wrong places. Not broken, just …

Cavell turned to Younker. "I don't think I can—"

"Come on, Cavell, get a pulse on the bitch. Hurry up! I—"

Younker stopped in mid-sentence. His eyes left Cavell's face and looked up, up, far over and behind Cavell's head, as Cavell sensed, but did not see, something rising tall, too tall, behind him.

"Younker?"

Younker breathed in. Breathed out. Breathed in again, then opened his mouth for a bellowing scream that came out silent, like air in a great hollow tunnel.

Cavell turned.

The bloated, dark shape swung down and bit him quickly on the neck, twice, before running back up its silk line, scuttling across the ceiling, and falling on Younker like a leaden weight. Immediately Cavell felt ice in his veins as the poison pulsed into his body. His face and shoulders already numb, he could hear Ms. Burgett working behind him, but could not turn. All he could see was the mass of tiny, brown spiders seething across the webs of yarn and over a wet, deflated mess that had disguised Ms. Burgett well for a long time.

A touch of something thin and sharp behind him, and he found himself turned about to face her again.

Your children, Cavell mouthed silently as she spun her webbing tightly around him with hairy spinnerets. No more yarn, now.

"Adaptable!" Younker shrieked beside him. "I'll give you that! All these years. Good for you! You had me fooled. You had…"

Younker's face went slack. He spoke no more.

Ms. Burgett, Cavell mouthed. *Ms. Burgett, please.*

"*Mrs.* Burgett," she snarled, looming over the stricken man. The voice from the wide, slavering mouth was like night wind hissing through dead grass. She dipped her fangs toward him again, hairy pedipalpi caressing his face, the red hourglass on her raised black abdomen shining wetly in the dim fluorescent light, and added, "*I'm a widow.*"

The Day After

Christmas Day was sixteen hours over. Presents lay open and scattered across three cluttered rooms. The house was full of people sitting in scarred furniture, smoking cigarettes, drinking beer, eating cold ham and warm chicken salad. Cats snaked around the legs of children. Children ran into adults, bumped their heads, cried. On the floor of the kitchen, in front of the dishwasher, a black poodle puppy with a red bow around its neck slept soundly, oblivious to the nearby trampings and voices.

One of the men at the kitchen table, fifty-two years old, had just arrived. The engine of his white Toyota Camry still ticked with heat by the ice-slicked curb. His wife, prim in a tan turtleneck and red wool sweater, sat beside him, making small talk with his sister. Outside, on the front porch, his son smoked a cigarette next to strange relatives and stared at the ground.

The man had been in the house a month ago for Thanksgiving and four months before that for an unexpected visit. Beyond that, he seldom saw the place. He lived far away.

Although eight people sat crammed around the table and half a dozen children crawled and toddled across the linoleum floor, the man was only concerned with one person: the old woman sitting across from him.

She had no teeth because she refused to wear her dentures and her hair was long, straight, and white. Although almost blind, she didn't wear glasses. That was something else she refused to do.

The man reached over an ashtray filled with cigarette butts and beer tabs. He took the old woman's palsied, wrinkled hand in his own. She clutched it with surprising strength.

"I went to Spain last week, Mum," the man said at last. "Did I tell you that before?"

"I don't think so."

"It was beautiful," he said.

"Oh yes?"

"Yes."

Both of them fell silent, but neither let go of the other's hand. Kaitlyn, the eight-year-old granddaughter of the man's brother, ran into the kitchen and demanded someone play Hungry, Hungry Hippos with her. She threw the game up on the table until someone did. The marbles made loud rattling noises until the man's wife lost to her. Then she dragged it off the table and ran out of the room.

"Jeff's doing well in school," the man said to the old woman.

"What?"

"Jeff's doing well in school."

"He must be in high school now."

"Actually he's in college, Mum. Remember?"

"Oh, yes. Yes, of course."

"He's a junior. He even has an apartment downtown. He can walk to all his classes. He's doing really well."

"That's good. That's very nice."

Out of the outdoor cats, a white shorthair the size of a Shetland Sheepdog, had found its way inside and into the kitchen. The man's sister-in-law screamed at it, then screamed at one of her daughters to throw it outside. The daughter told her seven-year-old daughter to do it for her. The seven-year-old grabbed it and carried it out of the room by its armpits. She returned a moment later with a four-inch scratch on her arm, bawling her head off.

Together, mother and daughter went off to the bathroom. The man's sister-in-law shouted medical instructions from across the house.

The man tried again.

"I remember when John and I were kids," he said. "Remember how we used to make Christmas ornaments out of papier-mâché?"

"Um."

"We used to make two dozen at a time, all shaped like stars, then sell them door-to-door. Remember that? We used to sprinkle them with glitter."

"Oh. Oh, yes. Sure."

The old woman fiddled with her empty teacup. She picked it up off the saucer, looked inside, and set it down. Then she picked it up again and started clinking it against the saucer. She clinked it so rapidly the man couldn't keep track of it. Then she stopped and placed it gently on the table beside the saucer, running a yellowed thumbnail along its cracked rim.

"Janet and I both have next week off," the man said. "It feels good to have some time away from work. We've both been so worn out."

"Oh, yes."

The man nodded.

The old woman's gaze rested on her teacup again. She picked it up and started clinking it against her saucer a second time. Then she stopped abruptly and looked him in the eye. "I have to find my keys. It's late and I'd better be getting home now."

"Mum, you are home," the man said gently.

"This isn't my house."

"You've lived here for three years. Remember? You live with John now."

The old woman shook her head violently. "No I don't. I live on the farm. They must be getting tired of me. I've been here all day."

"Mum, it's okay. Don't worry. It's okay."

A paused lengthened between them. Everyone else kept talking, but they did not.

"I'm sorry," the old woman said at last. "I get confused by things."

"It's not your fault," the man said. "Don't worry. It's just how things are."

The old woman looked at the man and smiled. The man squeezed her hand and she squeezed back.

"You remind me of my son," she said.

In the other room, one of the little boys knocked over a glass of Pepsi. Everyone in the kitchen knew it was Pepsi because three other children came in and started yelling about it.

Come Spring

They tramped up the back yard, through the woods, to the clearing at the top of the hill. It was very steep and the dew-wet grass made each step tricky, so Jake grabbed his grandfather's hand and held it tight.

"You tired?" his grandfather asked.

"Course not, Grandpa. You?"

"No siree." Sweat ran down the wrinkles of the old man's face and into his white beard.

"I never been this high up above town before," said Jake.

"It's a special place," said his grandfather, stopping to catch his breath. "Whenever a forest ends somewhere up high, you know you're in for a sight. And beyond the hill, far down below, there's a stream where I used to fish when I was a boy. Caught trout the size of my forearm!"

Jake stared at his grandfather's forearm, trying to picture it.

"Can *we* go fishing there someday?" he asked.

His grandfather didn't answer, just stared up the grassy slope. After a moment he reached into his jacket pocket and pulled out his pipe.

"Don't tell Grandma," he said, and struck a hidden match off his thumb.

Jake, impressed by this profound and casual trick, forgot all about fishing for the time being.

They continued climbing. "Can you do that again?" he asked.

"Sure can," his grandfather said, then leaned over and snapped fire off the brim of Jake's cap.

"There used to be butterflies here in the summer," his grandfather said. "Huge. Some yellow and black, some red, hard as all get-out to catch."

"Did you ever?"

"Sometimes. Had a big case full of bugs when I was your age. Maybe I can help you start your own. We can make a case out of some pine scraps I got in the shed."

"Yeah?"

"Well sure, why not?"

They tramped on. The sun, bright and warm despite the early November morning, blazed down, and the wild grass began to dry.

Suddenly Jake remembered something he didn't want to remember. Without thinking, he stopped cold.

"What's the holdup?" his grandfather asked, turning back.

"Nothing," said Jake.

"Then let's go! Grandma will murder us both if we let breakfast get cold. We have to keep moving."

But Jake just stood there, grass up to his knees, looking up at his grandfather with different eyes.

"You feeling better now, Grandpa?" he asked quietly.

His grandfather puffed out a circle of silver smoke and smiled. "That what's bothering you?"

Jake nodded.

His grandfather nodded back. "Well," he said, spitting expertly out the side of his mouth, "That's a funny thing. Funny odd, I mean."

He looked around for a place to sit down. Off to his left, the old stump of a once-enormous tree lay like a flat, smooth rock in the grass. He eased himself down slowly, motioning for Jake to sit beside him.

"This heart," he said, poking his chest casually with his pipe, "is what all the trouble's over."

"Is that why you had to go to the hospital over Christmas?"

"That's right."

"And did the doctors fix it? Is it OK now?"

His grandfather stared at him evenly for what felt like a long time.

"You having a good morning so far?" he asked.

"Sure am," said Jake, "but I'd have a better one if I knew you were doing OK."

"You don't like liars, do you?"

Jake thought about it. "No sir," he said. "You said not to take truck with liars."

"Well, I guess I had a point there." Chewing on the end of his pipe, the old man seemed to balance two things in his mind.

"No," he said at last.

"'No' what, Grandpa?" asked Jake.

"No, the docs couldn't fix it," he said.

Jake, shocked, felt tears well up.

His grandfather smiled and let out a dry laugh. "Well goodness gracious, Jake, that's all right."

Jake shook his head. "No! No, that's not right at all! How can you *say* that, Grandpa?"

"Well, I'm here now, ain't I?"

Jake said nothing.

"*Ain't* I?" his grandfather demanded.

"Yeah, Grandpa. You're here now. But you—"

"Won't be soon?" The old man tamped out his pipe on the stump and put it back in his pocket. He ground out a last bit of smoldering tobacco with a calloused thumb. "That what you mean to say?"

"Yeah," said Jake.

"We'll see," said his grandfather, squinting up the hill into the bright sun. "Come on, now. I was honest with you, you've got the truth, but for now we've got a good day ahead of us. That's what's important. No matter what, we can't let it go to waste. I do so hate a ruined day."

The old man slowly eased himself up off the stump and started climbing the hill again. Jake stood behind him, staring at the familiar figure but not moving.

"Come on, Jake! Don't you want to see the view?"

A fast decision made, he ran to catch up. A moment later he met his grandfather on top of the hill and gazed out at a wilderness of golds and greens and browns and reds, all glistening and brilliant in the early morning sun.

Far below, in the valley, a silver thread of stream wound its way from someplace out of sight to someplace out of sight.

"Is that where you used to fish?" Jake asked, pointing.

His grandfather took a moment to answer; he was gasping for breath.

"That's where I used to fish," he said in a hoarse voice.

"Can we fish there together sometime?" Jake asked for the second time that day, taking his grandfather's hand again.

"Why...why sure we can. Sometime we can fish there together. Come Spring. When the fish come out of hiding."

"Promise?"

His grandfather looked down at him and smiled. "What did I say about having truck with liars?"

Jake smiled back, squeezing his grandfather's hand tighter. Then he blinked. For a brief moment his mind had wandered.

He looked down at the child holding his hand.

"Grandpa Jake?" the child asked.

"What's up, Doc?"

"You feeling better now, Grandpa?" his grandson asked in a small voice.

Jake nodded, trying not to cough. When he started it was hard to stop.

His grandson tugged his hand. "Is that where you used to fish?"

Jake looked down at the stream far below, a ribbon of silver winding its way from someplace out of sight to someplace out of sight. "No," he said. "But I always wanted to."

"You wanna go fishing there sometime with *me*?" his grandson asked.

"Yes," he said, without hesitation.

"When?"

Jake smiled. "There's a good day ahead of us. We'll come back this afternoon. Pack a picnic lunch. I'll drive down to Stockton's and buy us some gear first."

"Really?" the boy exclaimed. "*Promise?*"

"I don't hold much truck with liars," Jake said, then closed his eyes and breathed in the smell of spring.

Wolf Stone

Brewster was melancholy—a vague adjective which can mean anything from mildly glum to virtually suicidal. His case fell somewhere in between.

"Melancholy" usually conjures up mental images of an ennui-stricken consumptive from the nineteenth century. Brewster was luckier—a twenty-first century college graduate, physically fit, education paid for and completed, and more than a little spoiled by doting, upper-class parents. But his degree in eighteenth-century European theater was worse than useless; it was pointless. Everyone had told him so from the start, but after five years spent working as an assistant manager at Blockbuster Video with no brighter job prospects in sight, no lasting relationship, and no greater understanding of the world around him, he'd finally come around to admitting it to himself.

So in a listless, self-pitying state of mind Brewster sold his apartment in Killington, moved back in with his parents, and wondered what to do next. Not finding any ready answers, he started losing weight, stopped shaving, didn't bother washing his clothes, and seldom left the house. He made a nest for himself in the basement, complete with television, couch, computer, and mini-fridge… and there he hid.

Three weeks after the return, his father came downstairs.

"You should go back to the doctor. He helped you before."

"No."

"Then you're going to Aunt Margaret's."

"Aunt Margaret's dead," said Brewster.

"Very observant. But the house is still there, and you're going to spearhead a restoration operation. That's lakefront property, prime real estate. You're going to have the place inspected, hire contractors, live there while the work is underway, make sure nothing gets stolen—"

"I don't want—"

"And get your shit together while you're at it." He patted Brewster on the shoulder and clumped back upstairs.

* * * * *

There wasn't much to do in Bethany. All the wonder from Brewster's childhood visits to his aunt's had died with her. Lake Erie still held some appeal, but autumn pushed him away from dark water and the darker thoughts that came with it. While the contractors worked, he walked. Too much noise to watch TV. Too much sawdust and commotion to sleep.

One of his only mildly satisfying discoveries was the Bethany Historical Society, an old three-story clapboard built in the 1880s. Except for Stockton's Grocery and Drug, the post office, Paige's Pizzeria, and a VFW hall, it was about the only building in town open to the public.

He signed in at the front desk, much to the delight of the blue-haired woman behind the counter, and declined a guided tour for two dollars—much to the woman's obvious dismay. After falling back into sullen silence, she returned to her faded paperback and ignored him completely. This left him free to explore in a bored, haphazard way.

It was on the third floor, under the slanted attic eaves, that he found the portrait. Stacked among photos of the Bethany Flood, he almost overlooked it, but a hint of color—of *skin*—caught his attention among all the black and white.

The frame, too, was different from the rest—ornate gilt and arabesque patterns instead of unpolished oak. He turned it over. A date on the back, in flowing quill pen: *1792*.

A sharp breath of air cleared away the heavy cover of dust. Brewster stared at the young woman and she stared back. Her eyes, a faded green similar to his own, gazed at him with playful vitality. A pile of red hair, held in place with jeweled combs, accentuated the pristine, almost translucent ivory of her skin. *She can't be more than twenty*, he thought, *and she knows what that means…all those years stretching ahead. So much time. So many possibilities. Look at that poise, that confidence…*

Embarrassed, surprised, he found tears verging in the corners of his eyes. Worse, he heard footsteps on the stairs. Clearing his throat, he looked at the portrait with close interest, trying to regain his composure. Doing so, he was surprised to notice that the girl didn't have any teeth. She was smiling—grinning, actually—but the artist had chosen to leave a swath of pink acrylic gum lines where her teeth should have been.

The woman with the blue hair waddled up behind him. "Closing in ten minutes!"

"Oh yes…I'll be going."

She peered over Brewster's shoulder.

"That's not supposed to be out for public viewing," she said in an accusatory tone.

"Sorry. I didn't know."

"Not your fault. Bernice, the other guide…she's always moving stuff around. Should be back in the basement. No one wants to see *that*."

"It's a good painting. Was she one of Bethany's first citizens?"

"Who, Roberta Kirkpatrick?" She snorted.

"Is that her name?"

"Sure is. Was. No, the town's far older than her. If you'd taken the *guided* tour, you'd know that."

"Oh. Yes."

"No, she was just a girl who died young. Lots of those back then. Nothing special."

"What happened to her teeth?"

The woman leaned in close. "Don't know," she said, recoiling quickly.

"How'd she die?"

The woman looked at her watch. "Closing time!"

* * * * *

Brewster couldn't get the portrait out of his mind. Or the name. "Roberta Kirkpatrick," he whispered that night in the dark, as the wind clattered tree branches above the house and pushed waves against the shore of the lake. She fascinated him—close to his age, but separated by over two hundred years.

In the morning he walked up Bethany Hill to the end of the paved road. A half-mile up the steep dirt path beyond, he came to the old cemetery. Forty-five minutes later he was kneeling in the dead grass by Roberta Kirkpatrick's grave. The chiseled letters on the headstone were almost worn away, but the massive slab of granite that lay across the length of the grave bore a deeper inscription, along with two dates: 1773-1794.

"She was twenty-one," Brewster murmured.

"Twenty," said a voice behind him.

He whirled, heart slamming.

An old man stood behind him, smiling apologetically.

"Didn't mean to startle you," said the stranger. "I keep a home over the crest of the hill. Watch over the graves. Stupid kids come up once in a while, especially round this month when it's close to Halloween. Do all kinds of mischief if you let 'em."

"I just came to look for her," said Brewster, nodding at the grave.

The old man clucked his tongue. "Name's Dwight Farnum. You from around here?"

"My Aunt was Margaret Peron."

"Oh hell, I knew her! Fine lady. Nobody never said a bad word about her. You selling the property?"

"Yes."

"Damn shame. You know, I used to—"

"Do you know anything about *her*?" Brewster interrupted, pointing to the stone.

Farnum paused, rubbing the back of his sunburned neck. "Well...not much," he said slowly.

"I saw a portrait. How come she didn't have any teeth?"

Farnum's face drained of color so fast Brewster thought he'd have to save him from a fall.

"There was a good reason," Farnum said thinly, steadying himself, "but I can't rightly remember what it was."

"You don't look so good. Here, sit down on the slab a minute."

"I won't sit on no wolf stone," said Farnum quickly. "And I'm fine, thank you very much. I'd best get on. You keep away from here, now."

And Brewster, too surprised to speak, could only shake his head while the old man walked away.

* * * * *

That afternoon, Brewster looked up "wolf stone" on Google.

"A slab of concrete or stone placed on a grave to keep wild animals from disturbing the remains of the recently interred," he murmured. "Popular through the mid-nineteenth century."

The rest of the evening Brewster felt increasingly anxious. He hadn't had a monomaniacal impulse since high school, but he recognized the signs that he was now in the grip of a developing obsession. He struggled against it for hours, but couldn't shake the thought of Roberta Kirkpatrick's body beneath that massive slab; of her decay; of her skeleton surrounded by stained, disintegrating burial cloth. Alone, far from anyone he knew, she felt like a friend, and he grieved for her passing.

He missed her.

He thought of her wolf stone. What a terrible necessity—a monstrous reminder of a long-gone culture's fear. Images of corrupt, defiled graves coursed through his mind. And wolves, of course. They skirted his thoughts like dark figures on the edge of firelight.

Later, in tormented sleep, Brewster tossed and turned, haunted by dreams of Roberta's face. The eyes, the hair, the smooth marble skin... even the toothless mouth didn't detract from her striking beauty. That face promised great things—friendship, love... *other* things; fulfillment in all its great and many forms...

He woke up bathed in sweat, loins throbbing, eyes wet, and knew his father had been right to send him here. And he continued to know this as he threw on his clothes, went out to the shed in the back yard, grabbed a crowbar and shovel, and trotted silently up Bethany Hill.

"There are no wolves now," he said, digging around the base of the slab as quietly as he could. "No wild animals." He giggled. "All dead. All dead."

He pressed down on the crowbar with all his weight, heaved at it until a blood vessel burst in his left eye, and laughed wildly as the wolf stone moved an inch, then two.

"You called to me the only way you knew how," he whispered two hours later, three feet down in the grave, "and here I come."

Soon the coffin, surprisingly intact, began to take form beneath the dirt. His shovel struck old sheet metal.

"Roberta," he said, and dug at the box with his nails. Earth fell away in wormy clods. The rotting casket lay fully revealed. He pulled a flashlight from his back pocket, turned it on, and clamped it between his teeth. He reached up for the crowbar, eyes wide, smiling with expectant glee.

"My purpose," he whispered, and forced open the coffin.

* * * * *

The heart attack that killed Dwight Farnum came two weeks after he found the young man's body, but nobody doubted that the shock of the discovery contributed heavily to his demise.

Just days before his death, Farnum drove down to Tap's Bar outside of town, a rare enough event, and when some of his cronies started asking questions he waved them down.

"I didn't come to talk, I came to drink," he said. "But all I'll say is that I never seen a body like that before." He downed a big gulp of lager. "Throat ripped out an' all."

"Police say it was like claws did it," someone said.

"My last words on the subject," Farnum muttered, setting down his empty mug and reaching for his hat, "are that Mr. Brewster learned three things. First, he learned why they took out that Kirkpatrick girl's teeth all them years ago. Second, he learned they probably should've taken out a few other things, too. And last of all, I guess he learned what a wolf stone's *really* for."

He tipped his hat and left the bar, which had gone very quiet.

And shortly thereafter, he died.

All, Always

Paul Burton sprouted up in a small town called Plumville, and in Plumville the Christmas season officially began on "Light-Up Night" down at the courthouse, where a few dozen strands of colored lights sparked off a speech by Mayor Davidson, two competing choirs, the train display down in the station shooting range, and an earnest bake sale by the formidable ladies of the Plumville Historical Society.

But for Paul, Christmas *truly* began when his father and mother piled him and his sister into the old Ford truck and headed out to the McCullough farm to choose the family Christmas tree.

Choosing was a laborious process. His mother always wanted a *thin* tree, his father always wanted a *fat* tree, Janey always wanted a *little* tree, and he always wanted the biggest one they could fit in the house. Beyond that, the pros and cons of ten-dozen Frasier Furs, Douglas Furs, Blue Spruces, and White Pines had to be weighed, debated, and argued over.

Ultimately, the final decision was based on compromise—and a "thinnish chubby tree, not too tall," was invariably purchased, tied to the back of the truck, and driven home. Once the roots were tied up in plastic and the tree balanced up, they decorated it with homemade stars, cranberry garlands, silver tinsel, bubble lights and winking lights, white lights and colored lights. Then Mom heated up cinnamon cider and cooked sweet and sour beef-log, and Christmas was officially under way.

So it had gone when Paul was two, six, twelve, twenty-four, thirty-two, and all the in-between years that, once past, weave together into a glowing sheen of memory. But his mother's passing, shortly before his thirty-third Christmas, had marked the beginning of the end—a time of downward-spiraling change that destroyed ritual and froze warmth. Crisis followed crisis, and now, six days before his forty-fifth Christmas, there *was* no tree—only a hospital room.

"Dad," he said, gently shaking his father's shoulder. The skin felt warm and dry through the thin paper gown.

"Mmmm." The old man opened jaundiced eyes and peered out at the small world of pastel walls and mildly alarming plastic machines that counted down his life.

"Dad, I have to go now. I wanted to say goodbye. I'll be back first thing tomorrow morning."

For a long moment Paul's father didn't seem to comprehend what he was saying, or even realize he had spoken. It was hard for Paul to tell. Paul cleared his throat, opened his mouth to repeat himself, then stopped as his father raised a hand.

"Janey," a broken-reed voice said.

Paul sighed. "Sorry, Pop. I tried every number I had. I called Information, old friends… I even contacted Bob."

"Bob's a son-of-a-bitch." The disused voice gained confidence. "If I'd known what he was really like, I never would have let Janey marry him. And if she hadn't divorced him, I would've killed him myself."

"I know. And he hung up on me, so that didn't help."

Paul's father grinned. "Almost Christmas and our holiday sucks. Ho ho ho!"

He smiled back. He couldn't help it.

The old man chuckled. "Not much fun, is it? Your mother gone, me on the way out, your sister MIA, you divorced. Shit. What are you going to do? Who are you going to spend Christmas with?" He held out his hand. Paul took it. The skin was like tissue paper. The grip was palsied but oddly, desperately strong.

"It doesn't matter, Pop." The words were listless and hollow, dark emptiness behind false nonchalance.

Paul's father snorted. "Sure it does. I'm stuck in this bed, but *you're* not. I don't want you moping around, even if there *is* plenty to mope about. I got you a present. I think you'll like it. If you do, then I know you just as well now as I did when you was a little kiddo. You always loved Christmas."

"That's right. It used to be my favorite holiday."

"Mine, too. And it still is. So listen up. In my bathrobe—"

A nurse bustled in, humming, and administered a shot. The old man gave her a dirty look, began to extend his middle finger, then sank abruptly into a deep sleep. The hand that held Paul's relaxed its grip slowly, a worn bundle of bones and sinew.

Paul placed it gently on the coverlet over his father's chest, then quietly left the room.

* * * * *

He threw his keys down on the coffee table and collapsed into an easy chair. The apartment didn't feel like home. Outside, Pittsburgh hummed with late-evening life. Inside, sterile walls, much like those of the hospital he had just left, stared blankly back at him and did not comfort.

Paul liked to talk, but since his divorce and his father's illness had forced the move from his town and house, there hadn't been many people to talk to. So he talked to himself.

"This isn't Christmas," he told the dark television screen.

He got up and made himself a cup of instant coffee, took one sip, and splashed the rest in the sink. He took a shower, shaved so he wouldn't have to do it in the morning, wiped the foam off his face, and stared at the medicine cabinet mirror.

"I can't remember what Christmas was like," he said softly, looking into his own hollow eyes. "I know it was good, I have the memories, but the feelings are gone." He dropped his head, and when he raised it again the face that stared back at him was very pale. "It's like all those Christmases happened to someone else. Or like they never happened at all."

The telephone rang in the other room. After staring at himself for a moment longer he went and answered it, and learned that his father had died in his sleep.

* * * * *

"In my bathrobe."

The words haunted him as he drove back to the hospital in the freezing rain. They haunted him as he stepped through the hospital's sliding doors. They haunted him in the elevator, in the hallway, in the room with the empty bed.

They haunted him as he reached into his father's bathrobe, still hung up on the hook in the tiny closet, and slid a hand into the pocket.

They haunted him as he pulled out a piece of paper and unfolded it.

He read the letter in his father's shaky print, re-read it, put it in his pocket, then went to take care of all the details that suddenly rear up to confront the grieving when someone dies.

* * * * *

On December 25, Paul drove the three hours to Plumville. He rented a room with Mrs. Diller, his old piano teacher who now owned a bed & breakfast, and let her make him a nice lunch. He sat down and ate it in the deserted common room. Then, as dusk began to fall and a few stray wisps of snow took flight on the cold, gentle wind, he donned his hat, buttoned up his coat, and stepped out onto the sidewalks of his old hometown—a tiny Western Pennsylvania hamlet slowly fading away as the abandoned coal mines lost definition and caved in upon themselves, dotting the landscape with sinkholes.

After two blocks he stopped walking. In the light of one of the town's telephone pole Christmas stars, he unfolded his father's letter and read it for the tenth time:

Paul,

Go to Plumville. Rent a room with Mrs. Diller, let her make you a nice lunch, then, when night begins to fall, walk over to the old house, up the back yard path, and into the woods. Remember when we used to walk in the woods after Christmas dinner? Once you hit the old train tracks, turn left and keep going till you reach the station house. I bought it years ago. It's yours, but that's not the present. Your present is inside. And outside.

Pop

Paul folded the letter again and walked up the driveway of a small, abandoned house, empty ever since his father had moved into the nursing home in Pittsburgh four years before. The windows were broken, black and vacant like empty eye sockets. Inside, the rooms that had hosted his youth lay in deep shadow, wallpaper peeling, floors warping without the century-long treads that once kept them flat.

He walked up the river stone path his father had built by hand fifty years before. Shivering, he stepped under the first of the trees that flanked the end of his old back yard. Deep, deep in on the old trails, then to the rusted tracks and left, on and on, the cold creeping into his blood, the darkness almost alive, the woods immense and silent, everything brooding above the small, warm town below. And then the station house, faded green shingles and wooden slats framing a door that opened like a dark mouth into gloom.

"Why," Paul murmured, "did he bring me all the way out here?"

He snapped on a flashlight, unlocked the door, and stepped inside.

Dust lay thick on a creaking, empty slat floor. In one corner a small desk stood next to a stuffed outdoor rocking chair. On the wall, above the desk, was a red fuse box. A sign attached to it with masking tape read, "OPEN ME." Paul did. Inside was a single switch. Paul's breath smoked hotly on the freezing air and hitched hard in his throat. He flicked the switch up.

The world blazed with light.

It took him a moment to figure out where it was coming from. Then he did.

Paul stepped back outside into a forest of evergreens, each one decorated with thousands of lights, strand upon strand, color upon color, a glowing wonderland in the middle of cold, darkened wilderness. Some of the trees were stately, tall, and full-bodied. Others were younger—smaller, shorter, and more recently pruned.

In the thin winter breeze that moved and shifted the lights in a kaleidoscope of branches, Paul stumbled forward. He leaned down by the base of a particularly large pine and shone his torch on a small brass plaque nailed to a stand.

Christmas 1971, it read.

Paul shook his head. He moved on to one of the smaller trees. It, too, was marked.

Christmas 2000, read the plaque.

He didn't understand. Blinking rapidly, he returned to the station house to look for a clue. He found it on the table below the fuse box—a thin slip of paper with his name on it, covered in dust.

Written in his father's hand, but in stronger script, before he became ill, the message was short and simple:

Paul,

These trees grew for me. Now they grow for you. They are all here, always.

Pop

And suddenly a gear clicked into place in Paul's head and it all made sense. He ran back outside in a fever, cold and warm, jaw slack and tight, slack and tight.

"All our Christmas trees. Every single one. From every year."

He stared out at the illuminated forest and said nothing else. His father had always brought their Christmas trees home alive, roots and all. No one ever questioned why or what he did with them after Christmas, when the chore of taking down decorations distracted them with melancholy. "Just another late December afternoon," Paul had thought on such days, "and Christmas so far away again."

But it hadn't been. No, not at all.

A gentle snow began to fall. A great deal gathered on Paul's hat and shoulders before he turned off the power in the station house and hiked back to town.

* * * * *

Mrs. Diller found him in the living room, feet to the crackling fireplace, a mug of hot cinnamon cider steaming gently by the arm of the overstuffed rocking chair.

"Mr. Burton!" she exclaimed. "Oh, I hope you haven't been alone long. I was over at my niece's for Christmas Dinner, and time slipped by so *fast*."

Paul grinned. "Don't think anything of it. I made myself nice and comfy."

Mrs. Burton paused, opened her mouth, shut it, then pursed her lips. Clearly, she wanted to say something. Finally she said it.

"Paul, it's none of my business, but you didn't spend Christmas all *alone*, did you?" Apparently she decided she had gone too far. "No, forgive me, don't answer that. It's none of my business. It's just… family makes all the difference sometimes. Even a quick visit or a phone call. Don't you think?"

"I couldn't agree more."

"Well … I hope you got to see or talk with your family today. Here, I'll go get us some Santa cookies." She bustled out of the room.

Paul, staring into the fire, nodded distractedly. "Yes," he responded once she was gone. The warm room embraced his voice. "I saw them, talked with them. It was quite a day."

He smiled, raising his mug. "What a gift."

Steel

In the early dawn light, Jacob Fields felt a hand on his shoulder and rolled over in bed to see what it wanted.

"Five o'clock," said his father. "Get up."

"I don't want to go."

"You're going," he said firmly. "Meet me outside in ten minutes."

Jacob took his time. He clumped downstairs eight minutes late, eyes sullen and fixed on the floor.

"Too late for breakfast," his father said from the kitchen. "Gear's in the back of the truck. Let's go."

Outside, Jacob changed into his camouflage jumper and orange vest in silence. His father looked on appraisingly. They climbed into the truck and his father gunned the engine to rattling, spluttering life.

Jacob's father had built his house on the edge of a long tract of forest in Western Pennsylvania, three miles from the nearest village and its silent, crumbling coal works. He drove them deeper into the trees, into true, rarified backcountry. The paved road soon turned to gravel, then dirt.

After a long silence, he jabbed Jacob in the side with a stubby index finger. "You like nature, kiddo. You'll like this. I got a blind nailed up in an old oak tree so hard to find nobody knows where it is except me. Real natural. You'll see."

"I'll sit there but I won't shoot," Jacob said softly. "You can't make me."

His father slapped him hard across the back of the head. "I want a dead deer, and I ain't doing no shooting today. Understand? We been through this before. No books this weekend. No goddamn flower walks. Jesus, thirteen years old and you've never even skinned a knee."

Jacob rubbed the back of his head and said nothing.

"Too bad there ain't a war with a draft on right now," his father continued. "World War II made men of a whole generation. So did 'Nam. On and on back, up to now. If I had any money, I'd truck you off to military school. Get your head of out the clouds. But this'll do just fine, I guess. Nothing quite like a good hunt. You wait an' see. It'll open up a whole new world for you."

Jacob opened his mouth to say something, closed it again, then said, "I never meant to make anyone ashamed."

His father grunted.

"I do real well in school. Mom taught me every day when I didn't understand something. I never get in trouble. Last year I won an art contest. They showed my painting at the mall."

His father sighed. "I don't mean to talk badly of the departed, kiddo. Your mother was a fine type, even though she treated me so shabby."

"She did *not*—"

"You did good by her," his father cut in, "but all those years without a man in your life—it ain't natural. Gives you no sense of yourself. You're getting your ass kicked at your new school twice a week, and we can't have that, can we?"

"It'll pass. They'll get tired of it soon."

"You need a little steel in your heart, kiddo. Something that won't bend to everyone else. This'll help give it to you. It'll be a start, at any rate."

Jacob opened his mouth to say more, but noticed that same steel in his father's face, in his gray eyes and hard mouth. Now, at least for the time being, he chose to keep his silence.

* * * * *

The blind was nothing more than a handful of boards tucked away in the upper branches of an old, lightning-struck oak. Covered with dead branches and camouflage canvas, it smelled of mold, decaying leaves, cigarette smoke, and dried whiskey.

"Now what?" Jacob asked, breathless from the climb up the half-rotten ladder.

"Now we have our quality time," said his father. "We wait for a deer and catch up on the last ten years."

But neither volunteered much, and so it had always been, ever since the funeral. Their lives, so different, refused to gel, even when forced to touch. Silence descended like a curtain between them, until the only sound was the ebb and flow of the forest—the minute resonance of flora and fauna that, combined, hum their routines out to the world.

Jacob's father pulled out a battered pack of cigarettes and flicked open a Zippo. Soon the acrid smell of stale tobacco cut an unnatural swath across the other scents of the wild. To Jacob, it was sickening; his mother had always hated it. Suddenly he missed her terribly, more than he had in the four months since her death, and he started to cry. He tried not to, but he couldn't help it. Everything was different. Everything was strange.

"Stop that." His father said it quietly.

He didn't.

"Stop that," his father said again. "You'll scare the deer."

An open hand cracked across his face. An angry red welt rose to throb tight and hot on his cheek.

Jacob stopped crying.

"That's what I mean," his father said, still in that soft, wooden voice Jacob could neither fathom nor penetrate. "Steel in your heart, kiddo. You need more than a little, but you ain't got none at all. Hey…"

He leaned over the blind, eyes squinted, peering out through the canopy.

"There." He pointed, then grabbed Jacob's shoulder and pulled him forward. In a slight clearing of fallen trees, a small doe ate calmly, quietly grazing among the ferns.

"Two-year-old if a day," his father muttered, reaching for his rifle. "You'll love the taste, Jacob. Meat tastes different when you kill it yourself. You *earn* it, then. It always tastes better when you earn it."

He proffered the rifle to Jacob, who shook his head.

"This ain't an option, Jacob."

"I'll miss on purpose."

His father's eyes were like slate.

"No you won't," he said. He turned, took careful aim at the deer, and fired. A jet of flame shot from the end of the rifle. The forest shook, the very air traumatized by heat and noise. Beyond it all, Jacob could hear intense silence, and as the echoes of the shot faded away, that silence took over, alive in the vacuum of life holding its breath.

Then, very faintly, leaves crinkled, ferns bent, as a small body fell among them and upon them.

Jacob stared out at the fallen deer. He bit his tongue until he tasted copper.

The deer wasn't dead. His father had shot it in the back flank, and it had fallen, too stunned to rise. It pawed the air feebly.

"It's suffering, Jacob," his father told him. "Let's go."

Jacob followed his father down the ladder and across the forest floor. In the clearing, the deer lay in a bed of blood-soaked fern, moaning softly.

Jacob's father handed him the rifle. He took it with numb fingers.

"You can't miss now," his father said. "Finish it."

Jacob shook his head.

"Finish it."

"No." A whisper.

"Finish it, Goddamn it! Finish it!"

Jacob aimed the rifle the way his father had taught him. A sob choked in his throat. He felt faint. *Steel*, he thought, and the image of his mother appeared behind his closed eyelids.

He fired.

Thunder rumbled across the land. The deer stopped moving.

"You did it!" his father exclaimed. "You did it, Ja—"

Jacob fired a second time. Then again. He riddled the deer's carcass. He squeezed the trigger, released, and squeezed until the last thunder died away and all the damage he could do was done.

Sounds of life returned slowly to the forest. His father stared at him. "You ruined it," he said softly. "Metal all through it. No one can eat the damn thing now. Goddamn it, Jacob!" He pulled his fist back to strike, then paused, breathing heavily. After a long moment the hand uncurled and fell to his side.

Jacob opened his eyes. He felt different. No tears welled up to fall. Slowly he bent down and picked a small cluster of yellow wild flowers from the forest loam. Not looking at his father, he placed them by the head of the still, silent deer.

He stood up and handed his father the rifle. Wordlessly, his father took it.

Without looking back, Jacob walked quickly out of the clearing, back to the path that led to the truck. He murmured something in parting.

"What's that?" his father asked sharply. "What you say, kiddo?"

"Steel," Jacob said a second time, louder than the first, and continued walking.

An Unknown Shore

It was a passion, and passions can never be fully explained. Why the Civil War? people asked. A hundred and forty years old and not getting any younger. Sure, a visit to Gettysburg is an eye-opener. Antietam Bridge is provocative. Harper's Ferry? A good way to spend a Saturday if it's not too hot. But why the full Union uniform? Why live in a tent ten weekends a year? Why the collection of bullets and bayonets, the library stocked with Shelby Foote and Walt Whitman, Sherman's memoirs and Lincoln's speeches?

There were many things Tyler Adams could have told them, but if they had to ask, there was no way they could ever fully understand.

But eventually, against all odds, he found a woman who *didn't* ask, who didn't mind pretending to be Clara Barton at reenactments and whose idea of a fun holiday was a weekend in old Richmond followed by a three-week voyage starting at Sumter and ending at Appomattox. Eight months later, Tyler married Paige Sayer and his life was finally full.

The Civil War. It had brought them together: Tyler a born-and-bred Bostonian, Paige a die-hard Savannah belle.

Yet now, ten years into a happy marriage, two weeks into a twenty-day battlefield tour, something happened that had never happened before.

"I think," Paige said, looking out at yet another of the endless strip malls between Antietam and Fredericksburg, "that I've had enough of the Civil War for awhile."

Tyler almost choked on his granola bar. "*What?*"

Paige turned and looked at him sadly. "Not forever, mind you. But for a little while. Perhaps a long while. We should spend the rest of our vacation elsewhere—someplace the Civil War never touched. Hawaii, maybe. Or Alaska."

"Secession!" he exclaimed.

Paige smiled. "Not quite as bad as that. It's just…" She broke off, face crumpling.

"Oh now," Tyler said, putting his hand on her arm. He pulled the car over and turned off the ignition.

"I feel… *too* close," Paige explained.

"To me?"

"No! Gracious, no. To *it*. To those four bloody years when the House was divided."

Tyler was silent. The car ticked in the hot day.

"It was Gettysburg that did it," she continued softly. "Time always seems *thin* there, have you noticed?"

He nodded.

"Like time is a veil, and all you need do is push it back…"

"Yes. Yes, I've felt it too. Many times. So much happened there, so much death and emotion, it's like a physical weight on the present. But Paige, we've been there *dozens* of times! Why now?"

"Because two days ago, when we packed our bags and said 'goodbye' to the Farnsworth House, that feeling *didn't go away*. Something followed us. Something that should be dead and buried and safely filed away in the history books. I wouldn't be scared, but… but…"

"But *what?*"

"But it's *inside* of me."

"What? What's inside?"

Paige took a deep breath. "Ever since Gettysburg I've felt things I've never felt before. Seen things I've never seen before. When I opened my eyes just now, I didn't see a paved highway... I saw a *dirt road*. And yesterday, when I woke up at the hotel in Antietam, I could have *sworn* it was a farmhouse, and that two horses stood waiting outside where our car should have been."

"Nonsense! You're just imagining things."

"*Am* I? I've never had a very vivid imagination, Tyler, but when we stopped for gas in York an hour back, I didn't see a service station, I saw a clapboard inn, and in front of that inn stood two dozen dusty Union Blues, dismounted, watering their horses. Three were wounded, bandages soaked with blood. And I could *smell* the horses, that sweet musky smell of hay and manure. I tell you, *it wasn't my imagination*."

Paige got out of the car. Tyler followed.

"And it's more than that," she continued, beginning to pace. "I'm not only seeing with someone else's eyes, I'm *feeling* someone else's *feelings*. Oh, the sorrow, Tyler. The *heartache*. We can never know what it was like to be a soldier then. Never. We *think* we can, and the feeling thrills us. But that's all. Never have I felt such despair as I have felt since leaving Gettysburg. And it is not my own."

She leaned against a rail fence a little way off the road and looked out on a field of golden wheat that stretched away into the distance.

"I don't know if I'm looking at a field now, in 2007, or a hundred and forty-five years ago," she murmured. "It's all too much. Can you understand that? Too much."

Tyler sighed. "I'm sorry," he said. "I brought this on."

"How can you say that? It's not your fault."

"There's a fine line between passion and obsession. We must have crossed that line somewhere along the way, and this is the result. All those reenactments. Those were my idea."

Paige shook her head. "You didn't force me to do anything. I've always loved this stuff." She paused. "You *do* believe me, don't you?"

"I believe you *think* you're seeing these things," Tyler said gently. "But they're not really there."

"But what about what I *feel?*" she demanded, voice rising.

"That's real enough, but it's *not* a ghost inside your head—"

"No," she interrupted, "It's a person from *another time*."

"—It's *you*," he continued, "overwhelmed by the magnitude of the tragedy."

She shook her head. "You don't understand."

Tyler raised his eyebrows. "Well, maybe not. But I think your idea is a good one. Let's use the rest of our vacation and go somewhere different. How about a cruise? Hawaii was a great idea."

* * * * *

Five days later, on the deck of a great ship plowing across the Pacific, Paige reclined in a chair and sipped a Cosmopolitan. The sun beat warm on her face. The breeze of the ocean cooled the warmth until everything felt just right.

"Three days until we reach Hawaii," Tyler said beside her. "This was a good idea. This was a very good idea. For us, for now, the war is over."

Paige nodded. The visions had almost ceased. Whoever it was that had traveled with her in her mind had all but packed his bags and left—headed, she hoped, back where he had come from.

Even so, something gnawed at her. Some other angle she hadn't considered. It didn't panic her like before, but nonetheless a small, distant worry remained.

"I wonder," she said softly. But Tyler, not hearing, left to find a magazine.

"I wonder," she continued to herself, "if what came with me from Gettysburg could look out of my eyes the way I could look through his? Time is thin there. And war divides some, yet brings others together. That's what history teaches. What visions did *I* give to *him*—whoever he is?

"And what, oh what, would he think of what he saw?"

She made no effort to answer her own questions. Putting on her sunglasses, she forced her mind silent, and focused instead on the incessant gold and white rhythm of the sunlit waves as they met with the distant horizon.

* * * * *

The man awoke suddenly in the pale sunlit room. Distracted, bemused, he dressed, washed, and descended the stairs to assume the duties of the day.

The Executive Cabinet awaited him in the morning room, seated around a long table of polished oak.

"You look tired, Mr. President," said Secretary of War Edwin Stanton.

The man rubbed his brow. "Gentlemen, several times in the last four years, always before some important event or disaster, I have had the same dream. I had it before Antietam, Fredericksburg, Gettysburg, and, lately, the surrender of Lee. I had this dream again last night."

He took a seat at the table. His deep-set eyes looked careworn and haunted.

"In my dream," he said slowly, "I stand upon the deck of a ship that is rushing on some vast and indistinct expanse…toward an unknown shore." He looked up with a tired smile. "I take it as a good omen, that perhaps reconstruction will commence quickly, and all animosity be buried in the efforts to come."

"Let us hope, sir," someone said, breaking the silence in the suddenly-quiet room.

"Yes," said the man. "But the dream does leave me tired. Well, tonight will bury that fatigue. Mrs. Lincoln and I will attend a performance at Ford's Theatre. General and Mrs. Grant may be joining us."

The cabinet then shifted to other matters, but all the rest of that day Abraham Lincoln appeared thoughtful, and sometimes raised his head—exactly, some reflected in the chaotic days that followed, as if looking toward a horizon he alone could see.

A Sense of Duty

The four men worked hard with handkerchiefs tied around their faces. The September floods had been very bad, the worst in a hundred years, and the graveyard by the woods outside town had paid the price. Now someone needed to clean up the mess.

"Ain't no work for a man," said one, shoveling clear a load of muck from the top of a disintegrating pine box.

"We volunteered, Hugh," said another. "It don't do no good to complain."

"We didn't volunteer for *this*, Carl," Hugh insisted.

"Stop your whining and shovel," Carl said, lifting the handles of a broke-down wheelbarrow full of bad earth and turning away with it. "Whining ain't fitting a man, neither."

"Carl's right," said the third. "Volunteer firemen are in for it, no matter the calamity. You signed up as a volunteer fireman, you volunteered for this. So here you are. It's for the good of the town... 'Course, it sure is nasty," he added, peering into the dank hole before him... mostly empty, but not quite.

"I guess, but it strikes me this here's a bit above and beyond the call of duty, or what have you," said Hugh. "You'll change your tune if you fall in there, Ted," he said.

The fourth man, the groundskeeper, returned from his trip to the storage shed, pulling an empty cart behind him. "That was Mr.

Wilbur Collins I just stored. Wiped off the name plate," he said. "The newer boxes all have 'em."

"Never did like Old Man Collins," said Hugh. "Shot me with rock salt once for cutting across his north pasture."

"How many we got in there now, Mike?" Carl asked.

Mike let go of the cart and wiped his brow with a gloved hand. "So far there's eleven… and some spare… odds and ends. Phew! For late September it sure is hot." He looked sick and pale.

"Eleven," said Ted, turning away from the open grave only to face another. Carefully, he picked his way back to clear ground. "That means," he continued once safe, "there's a good…well…"

"The chart says ninety-two," Mike said, rummaging in his overalls for a battered sheaf of papers. "Yep, ninety-two. But to be honest, this one hain't been updated in some time. The new chart, I'm afraid it was warshed away. Can't say as I can recollect all the names, seeing as I just took the post six months ago, but there's probably a few dozen more than what we see here."

"Jesus wept," groaned Ted.

"With all the stones strewn about, we got our work cut out for us," Mike agreed.

Hugh thumped Mike on the back, grinning. "Ain't you glad you got the job when you did?"

"Pineville's a small town, thank God for that," said Carl. "It could've been worse."

* * * * *

Around three they rested on a log at the far end of the cemetery, carefully checking before they sat to make sure there weren't any surprises lying nearby.

"Looking at it from this vantage point, I think I'm gonna cry," said Ted. "I don't wanna go back there."

From where they sat it became apparent just how little their day's work had achieved. One corner of the yard was mostly clear, tombstones neatly stacked against the low stone wall, nothing else in sight but a long hole every now and again or a bulge in the matted grass signifying a risen coffin the waters hadn't entirely freed.

The rest of the yard, sixteen square acres, was a charnel garden. Tombstones law strewn about, some face down, some face up, some cracked, some broken, some sticking in the earth by a corner after being tossed end over end by the current. Only a few of the heavier, expensive granite stones remained mounted and upright. In almost all cases the remains they memorialized were no longer where they belonged.

It was an old cemetery, some coffins planted so long ago there was nothing *left* to float, but Pineville had also been gifted with several generations of skilled casket makers who knew how to prolong disintegration and fit boards tight together; thus, many had risen when the waters called, only breaking open when those same waters currented them into trees, tombstones, rocks and each other. Scores of broken wood caskets littered the yard, along with their long-hidden contents that turned the stomach and watered the eyes…some still under lids, others strewn across the muck. Friends, family, and ancestors society had long ago accepted as lost had now returned, but they were not wanted.

"If only everything wasn't so *damp*," said Ted. "A little sun, a little heat—"

"Heat would only make it worse." Carl sniffed.

"But at least it would make everything less… less *dead*. I hate autumn. Cold mists, colder rains, and never enough sun. It's the sun I need more than anything. Besides, we won't be able to rebury any of these folk until the ground dries. We should pray for sun."

"Prayer is good, I won't argue none with that, but we should pray for strength more than sun," Mike said, "and hurry up and get on with our job before what strength we got left gives out." He stood, stretched, and trudged slowly back to his cart.

The others, equally slowly, followed.

"What we *should* pray for is a miracle," muttered Hugh, bringing up the rear. "Something involving me never having to see anything like this ever again."

* * * * *

By sundown the shed, formerly used for storing shovels, spades, hoes, rakes, bags of peat and wheelbarrows, now stored three dozen occupied coffins and the remains of a dozen and a half Pineville citizens without, the latter securely tied up in burlap sacks. Outside, four stacks of tombstones lay in front of the shed, to be sorted through and restored to their proper places later.

"Another two days should do it for the gathering," Carl said. "Then we can help Mike here with the sorting and put everybody back proper who can *be* put back."

The night was clear but moonless, the wind gentle but cool. They slept in Mike's cottage on the hill next to the shed, setting up two-hour shifts to guard the cemetery from animals that might worry the exposed remains. Mike lent out his rifle for the purpose, along with an oil lamp so no one would take any bad steps in the dark.

Carl picked the short straw and kept watch first. He walked the grounds carefully, handkerchief tied tight around his face, trying not to think. For two hours his only excitement was chasing a red fox away from what was left of Abigail Wilson. At two he gave Ted a kick in the leg and turned in.

Ted didn't go through the graveyard, just circled around it. He didn't want to stumble over any gaping holes in the dark, didn't even want to *risk* it, so he kept to the perimeter, scaring off rats and raccoons, then stumbling over, not a hole, but a wooden coffin that gave way as his boot pressed down.

Forty-five minutes later, still wiping his heel on the grass, he shambled, muttering, back to the house and woke Hugh.

Hugh chose sitting rather than walking, and parked himself on Mike's porch swing for guard duty. It was in pretty poor shape, the weather-worn wooden seat hanging from rusted chains which looked ready to break, but it felt good to sit, and everything held. In fact, it felt so good that after a while, probably not more than a couple of minutes, he drifted off into uneasy sleep.

He dreamt fitfully of mildewed linen, dank holes, and the sighing of fretting winds through dark tree boughs. The sound conjured images of waving doors that shouldn't be open; clattering attic shutters in abandoned mansions; cold, wet-ashed chimney flues… and after a time it grew louder, more distinct and insistent, until with a start and a cry he awoke.

But the sound did not cease.

"What's that?" he hissed, then clapped a hand over his mouth. "What *is* that?" he hissed again through white fingers. He looked back toward the front door and the black inside space beyond. Silence there, save for snores.

"Christ Almighty, that ain't *them*, he said, and fumbled for the dark lantern. "Gonna see," he said. "Gonna see what that goddamned sound *is*."

But he couldn't bring himself to strike a match.

The sound was like a tide, cries washing over voices, voices demanding answers. The sound was faint but resonated with the power of a multitude. Over the voices came the tread of feet on grass and leaves, the knocking of knuckles against wood, the ripping of fabric with fingernails.

"Lord a' mercy." The words could have been Hugh's but were not. They came from *behind* him. He spun like a top, arms raised to fend off or strike.

Carl grabbed him. "Now, now, it's just us." Mike and Ted stood beside him in the dark, holding their breath.

Together they stood on the porch and listened.

"It's coming from the bone yard," Mike whispered.

"Some of the kids from town come back to cause trouble?" Ted whispered.

"Hell no," Carl said. "No one would cause trouble with *that*." His shadow nodded toward the cratered lawn.

Mike took a deep breath and said, "Come on now, let's not get panicked. It's my job to see this property's residents are kept safe. I'm turning on a lamp." He fumbled with a match. Yellow flame sprang up, touched an oiled rope. The lantern glowed.

Hugh gasped. Ted shut his eyes tight. Carl grabbed the rifle from Hugh's hand.

Mike raised the lantern.

As though of the wind itself, the noise rose for a moment, then, protesting, faded quickly and completely away.

Nothing moved in the cemetery but rats and leaves.

Even so, no one caught a wink all the rest of that long night.

* * * * *

"Well, I'd say something looks different."

Everyone looked at Mike, who was surveying the cemetery, hands on hips and nodding slowly. "It don't look as messy today."

"That's cause we worked our behinds off yesterday," said Hugh. "Now my first order of business is to get that damned pine tree to give up her goods. It just don't look *right*, that thing all the way up in a tree." Shouldering a coil of rope, he walked over to the spruce planted in the middle of the lot and looked up into its cover, where the glint of a brass handle betrayed the presence of a coffin lodged between two branches some eight feet off the ground.

"I'd better help him," said Carl, following. "If the damn thing drops sudden it'll probably land on his head."

"Bag duty for me," said Ted, holding up a pile of burlap sacks with a grimace. "Gonna go in the woods and search for strays. Feel free to trade whenever you feel inclined."

"Gonna try and start matching pieces together, one stone to one coffin, one coffin to one body," Mike said, and went off to the shed.

The sun was bright and warm, good for drying out the earth but bad for what needed to be re-interred beneath it. They found their cologne-soaked handkerchiefs, tied them in place, and the work went on. There was no talk about the previous night.

Not until noon did something happen to put everything else on hold for a time.

It was Ted, out in the woods, who picked up on it first, and when he did he came running out from among the trees, waving his arms and wringing his hands. Everyone stopped and stared, and when he got close he called out, "There's a child in there! I can hear her crying!"

The search began immediately.

"No way anyone's in here," said Mike, turning to Ted as they picked their way among the trees. "You sure it wasn't a barn owl? They sound kinda like tikes when they're riled."

"Hey now, I know what I heard," Ted grumbled.

"It don't make no sense. The nearest farm—"

He was cut off by a wail the likes of which none of them had ever heard. It came from farther in the forest, but not too far, and worked its way into their bones until their footsteps slowed and they all grew still. It started high and ended low, but not low enough for an adult, and there could be no doubt it was a person. Ted was right. It sounded like a child, hurt and terrified.

"My God, that was it, that was the sound," Ted whispered, grasping Carl's arm.

"Leggo," Carl hissed. "Someone needs help." But for a long moment all they could do was stand in place looking toward the thickening cluster of pines that stood before them, and Ted held on.

The silence was deathly.

Then the cry went up again, the desolate wail of someone utterly lost and alone. "Mama!" that someone called. "Mama!"

It was Hugh of all people who was stirred into action by the sound. He was a father and knew *that* call of duty when he heard it. "Come on now," he said, and trotted off toward the noise. As if waking from a dream, Carl tore free of Ted's grasp and followed Hugh. Mike and Ted kept pace behind him.

Hugh moved rapidly, trying to pinpoint the location of the sound before it died away again. He pushed through the dead lower branches of some pine trees just as the wail was fading away, and arrived at the source of the sound before the last echo died.

There could be no doubt who had made it. The sound had led them to her, and they had found her.

The little girl in the faded pink dress lay in a shallow mud puddle in the shade of the trees, but there was no need to help her up. She had been dead for a long, long time. The skin of her face stretched tightly over her skull, dehydrated and tanned by long years underground. Her long, blond hair rested in dusty, disintegrating braids across her chest. Her hands were clusters of brittle white twigs. Her hollow eye sockets stared vacantly.

Around her lay the shattered remains of a small, white coffin.

Hugh let loose a yell that sent blackbirds flying off in fright. Mike and Ted simultaneously turned and were sick. Carl leaned against a tree, swallowed his risen gorge, and shut his eyes. When he opened them again he looked up and said, "The waters took her all this way. Guess it would be a good turn to take her back. Guess that's what she wants."

Like a funeral procession they filed slowly through the woods and back to the sun-struck graveyard, a small bundle in burlap carried between Carl and Mike. After depositing the bundle in the shed they went quickly back to Mike's house, trudged inside, and worked no more that day.

Later that night before they fell asleep in front of a cheery, popping hearth fire, Hugh sneaked over to the door and latched it tight.

No one asked where he had gone when he came back.

* * * * *

By morning they had collected themselves enough to return to work, and for the next three days labored diligently, ignoring flitting shadows and sheltering themselves at night by laughing too hard at jokes and sticking cotton in their ears when they slept. Although they remained on the property out of a sense of duty, they didn't keep watch on the grounds after dusk anymore.

They made fine progress. Soon all the "litter" was gone from the grounds and Mike began making a great many identifications, due in part to his own detective work, but mainly to a somewhat disturbing discovery he made one bright morning: during the night, someone had used a sharp stone, branch, or (here Mike shuddered, thinking of it) fingernail to scratch names onto all the coffins, and mud to write names on all the burlap sacks. Despite the issues this raised, it helped a great deal, and the four men figured that no matter how it had come to happen, the act was a gift.

One afternoon, after the reburials had begun in earnest, Carl was touching up a hole when he saw Mike sitting off by himself on a rock at the edge of the yard.

"Everything dandy?" Carl asked, but was taken aback by Mike's appearance. He looked sicker than any man he had ever seen. There was sweat on his forehead and upper lip, but Carl could tell it wasn't the good sweat of work, but the kind that comes with brain fever. He looked so pale the light seemed almost to shine through him, and his breathing was labored and loud.

"Lord a' mercy," Carl said, and put his hand out to touch Mike's shoulder. Mike shied away, and Carl withdrew with a raised eyebrow and a frown.

"You look sick, Mike. I don't know what to make of it, but I think you'd best get inside and lie down."

"I ain't *sick* sick," said Mike. "To be honest, right now I just want out of here for a bit. I want this over. I need time away."

"Well why don't you go, then?" Carl asked gently. "You've worked damn hard. No one can say different."

"Because if I leave now this job is history, and I need it bad. What with the Depression on, score's score of people ready to take over if I up and run, I'd be a crazy to walk away."

"Depression?" Carl said. "I don't follow."

Mike gazed at him long and hard, then motioned for him to sit down beside him. This time he didn't shy away.

"I found something 'bout an hour ago," Mike said.

"Yeah?" said Carl.

"I found the updated chart of the cemetery."

"Oh yeah?" said Carl.

"Just sittin' there right as rain, a little stained but still readable, right on top of my desk like it had been there all along." He pulled out a folded sheaf of papers from the front pocket of his overalls. "Here it is."

"Well that's fine, Mike, just fine. Now we can know for certain if we're missing anybody. But I don't see--"

"It'd please me if you took a gander at it. 'Specially the bottom of the second page."

Carl took the list, flipped to the second page, scanned it, and stopped short.

He breathed in and out, long and deep.

"My oh my," he said.

Mike swayed beside him, mopping his wet brow.

"Oh my," Carl continued. "Oh my oh my."

* * * * *

"What you need, Carl?" Ted asked. Several hours had passed. Carl had taken some time to collect himself, then gathered everyone together on Mike's front porch.

"Ted, Hugh, I got a question for the both of you. Before this job, what's the last thing you remember?"

Hugh snorted. "You drunk, Carl?"

"I just wanna know."

"Well…I…" He trailed off. "It's kind of hazy, now that you mention it."

"Ted?"

"Well hell, Carl, I guess my house and my wife and working in the mines. I got lotsa memories."

"I know you do, but what about *right* before? What do you remember about the flood? Who came and told you we needed to do this job?"

"Oh, now, Carl, that's easy … I mean … That is to say…"

Mike stepped in. "Hugh, what year is it?"

"1912," Hugh said immediately. "What the hell year you *think*?" He stood up. "You've all gone crazy, I –*ouch!*"

"Oh!" Ted grunted, grabbing his hand. "What'd you do that for?"

Carl held up a knitting needle.

"The year," Mike said flatly, "is 1934."

"Look at your fingers, fellas," Carl said.

The two men raised their fingers. Eyes, suddenly wide, suddenly terrified, examined them closely. A thick, clear liquid dribbled down both hands in slow rivulets.

"Embalming fluid," Mike said. "Unless I'm mistaken, I'm the only man here with a pulse."

* * * * *

There was a great stir on Mike's porch, and after the screaming and the exclaiming and the accusing and the shaking heads and frantic cries had ceased, three men walked the dirt road to Pineville and sought out their homes.

A short time later they returned, glassy-eyed and resigned.

"Now do you believe me an' Carl?" Mike said.

Hugh and Ted nodded their hanging heads. Their houses were abandoned, their families gone.

"What year you say this is again?" Ted asked quietly.

"1934," Mike said. "Pineville's been dead since the early twenties, when the coal gave out. I'm the only one here. All I do is tend the cemetery, see that no one bothers anything. Come from Pittsburgh, originally. Paid by the county."

They trudged back into the living room and slumped down in rocking chairs by the fire. Outside the wind blew cold, sending dried leaves scuttling across the porch boards and stressing the roof beams.

Mike said, "According to this chart, you all… er… passed away on the same date: May 23, 1912. You remember anything at all about it?"

They thought for a moment. "Come to think of it," Ted said, slowly, "I do remember something… something about water. But it's distant, like a dream."

"The mines!" Carl exclaimed. "Culver Lake. The flood."

"The roar… the rocks," said Ted.

"By God," said Hugh, "the collapse."

"We all work—or worked—the same midnight shift," Carl explained. "Looks like we didn't make it out of that one with all our faculties intact, as the doctors say."

Mike moaned. "This'll teach me for not taking an interest in other people's lives. If I'd only asked what you all did and where you all lived when you first got here...I just assumed you lived in Still Creek over the hill and were sent down to help. I never thought... that is, I never... I should have known when you was talking about Wilbur Collins. He died in 1893, and you all look so young, I—"

"Enough," said Carl. "Don't worry yourself over it. What we need to worry on now is the best course of action. There's something going on here that ain't natural, we've all guessed that since Day One, but now it seems we're a pretty big part of it ourselves. Well, to be frank I've got to say I don't think we belong up here, walking and talking, anymore than the rest of the folk out there who seem to be a tad restless too."

"Agreed," said Ted and Hugh.

"And I think we'd also agree that this is a fair bit, well, *upsetting* for us, what with us being dead and our families all moved on and away... upsetting for our friend here too, who ain't done nothing to deserve this kind of stress," Carl continued, nodding to Mike. "So the sooner things get back to normal, the better. Now, we've laid out there quiet for twenty-two years and change. Why we up and walking again now?"

"The flood," Hugh said.

"That's how I see it," Carl agreed. "The flood warshed us all up, something needed done to fix it, so we came back to ourselves. Taking care of this kind of thing is our job as volunteer firemen, after all."

"Agreed."

"But what about the others?" asked Ted. "Why are they up and about too?"

Mike said, "It's like that saying my granddaddy was fond of, the morbid cuss: 'The dead take care of their own.'"

"Sounds about right, given what's happened," said Hugh.

"Everyone out there in that yard and in that shed are doing their part, and we're heading up the project," Carl said.

"So all we got to do..." Hugh began.

"...is finish what we started, and things'll fall back into line around here." Carl turned to Mike. "After all this, you mind if we stay on at the house a little while longer? That fire feels good, even if we ain't supposed to notice such things in our condition."

"Well hell, boys," Mike said, and they were glad to notice the color had returned to his face, "I'd say you deserve that at the very least."

* * * * *

They had the cemetery back in good order at the end of two weeks. Some gravestones needed replacing including Carl's and Ted's (Hugh's was found in a rain gully a short distance from the grounds, a little chipped but otherwise fine), but Mike made a trip over to Still Creek and came back with a half dozen new stones. Finally, on October 27, they lined up in front of Mike's cabin and looked out upon the graveyard, grass neat, stones straight, and declared it finished.

All except one thing.

"Everything trim and tidy again, everyone tucked back in," Carl said. "Guess it's time you saw us off, Mike."

"Boys, it's been my pleasure." Mike shook hands all around. "You ready?"

They were. Three open graves lay side by side. Carl, Hugh, and Ted, dressed in smart, new tailor-made suits, climbed carefully down into the holes, minding the dirt, and lay down in the pine boxes they'd built for themselves the previous day.

"Feeling a bit tired, to be honest," Hugh said, reaching up to close his lid. "Miss my kids. Maybe if I go to sleep I'll see them again. So long, folks. Catch ya again sometime, I guess." He shut the lid, knocked twice, and Mike stepped down and latched it.

"I guess all this was fitting," Ted said, squirming slightly to get comfortable. "There ain't many people left to look after us... it would've been too big a job for you to do alone, Mike."

"You did great, Ted." The lid creaked shut. Mike latched it.

Carl shook Mike's hand again. "I want your honest opinion... you think this place looks good? Really good?"

"Even better that it did before."

"An untended grave is a shameful thing. It was quite a shock, this, but I'm glad we came back to do it." He reached up, grabbed the edge of his lid, and started to pull it closed over himself. "Oh, hey!" he added. "I almost forgot!"

"What's that, Carl?"

"We talked it over, and if you ever need any help keeping your house in good order—a paint job, new roof, whatever—don't hesitate, eh? We owe you."

The lid shut. Mike latched it.

Later, he found himself whistling as he shoveled on the dirt.

Welcome Home

The cat first appeared in the middle of winter. It came in the evening, after Scott Gardner finished shoveling the latest snowfall from the driveway so it wouldn't turn to ice. He wouldn't have noticed it if he hadn't heard the cries, but it was hungry, and cried to let him know.

"There's a cat under the car," he told his wife while taking off his boots. "Should we feed it?"

Emily's eyes brightened. "Do you really need to ask?" She went to the pantry, grabbed a can of cat food from a half-empty carton on the floor, and picked up a small blue bowl sitting next to it. She threw on a sweater.

Outside, shivering, she looked under the car, then all around in the falling dark. Nothing.

"I can't see under the car," she said. "Are you *sure* it's there?"

"Positive!" Scott called from the utility room. "It was *loud*."

"But did you see it?"

"Nope! But I know a hungry cat when I hear it—after Hider, I'd better."

Just then, the cat cried again. It sounded like it was under the car, but Emily couldn't be sure. Kneeling down, she peered into the oily shadows beyond the tires and saw nothing—but the light *was* fading.

She set the food out on the dry pavement beneath the eaves. Shivering, she closed the door.

* * * * *

Next morning the food was gone. Every bite.

"Should we put out more?" Scott knelt down and touched the light dusting of snow that had fallen during the night. "That's strange... no paw prints."

Emily shook her head. "No. We shouldn't have done it yesterday. I don't want to start that again."

"Start what?"

"You know."

"My allergies?"

She nodded.

Scott set the empty bowl back down. "Now that's not fair."

"No—it's just... with Hider, we fed him, we cared for him, but in the end we couldn't offer him a home. He cried to come in and we did nothing. And one February afternoon I found him dead in the road."

"Because we couldn't let him inside," Scott finished. "Because of my allergies."

"I don't want to get attached like that again. I know what will happen if I do."

She went back inside and closed the door—not angry, just resigned. And resolved.

Scott remained, staring at the slate-gray sky and bare, windswept trees. A gentle snow began to fall around him.

Great sadness descended upon him with the snow. Their twenty-year marriage had produced no children, and now, after a long season of growing unease, he recognized the missing element that had gnawed at them through all the seasons as their hairs slowly turned gray and their backs slowly bent: love between them was not enough. They needed something to love outside of themselves, something to care for that would care back gratefully and unconditionally, a give-and-take that left all for the better. A heart, however full, slowly goes bad without an outlet. Their hearts, however full, now needed release. But even something so humble as a cat was beyond their grasp—all thanks to his allergies: an inconvenience in his youth, a full and major setback now, as their capacity for love threatened to vanish with the last warmth of the dying year.

Without another thought, he went inside and returned a moment later with a can of cat food.

"There you are," he said, forking it into the bowl. "I can't see you, but at least I can feed you."

An hour later the bowl was empty again.

* * * * *

It was only after two weeks of clandestine feeding that Scott realized just how *odd* the new cat was—no paw prints was one thing: cats could step like feathers when they wanted. But to *never* see it? Several times now he'd heard it crying, meowing, purring—but could never place it. He'd searched all the possible hiding places, and nothing doing. Once, he'd left food, returned five minutes later to take the trash to the curb, and the bowl was already half empty. A moment later, walking back to the house, it had looked from a distance as if the rest of it was *disappearing before his eyes*.

It *can't* be, he thought at the time.

Now, however, he was seriously beginning to consider the possibility that it was.

Later that evening Emily walked into the den with a dazed, dreamy look on her face and said, succinctly, "I think I'm going crazy."

"You always say that," he said, not lifting his eyes from his book. Then, thinking back, he reconsidered. "Why?"

"Just now a cat brushed against my leg."

"And?"

"And nothing was there."

He sat up. "Where did this happen?"

"Outside. I was raking leaves."

Scott was silent a long, still time.

"Think I'm crazy?" Emily asked.

"No. No, I don't. That cat we fed a few weeks ago—it's... it's... I think it's a..."

He couldn't bring himself to say the word.

"I've been feeding it," he said instead. "I didn't tell you because you were upset about it before. I've never seen it, even after two weeks. And I *should* have. But it was never there. Or it *was* there, but... oh hell, you get my drift."

Emily went to the window and stared hard into the cold evening.

"You mad at me?" Scott asked.

"Yes," she said immediately, then turned. "Be sure to put out more food tonight. But put it in the parlor."

"Inside the house?"

"Inside the house," she repeated.

* * * * *

In the morning the food was gone.

The following evening something stepped up onto Emily's legs and into her lap so gently she wasn't even startled. For the next hour she sat with a rare smile on her face, watching television and petting the warm, invisible motor engine that rumbled contentedly on her lap.

"Why?" she asked later that night.

"I don't know," Scott said, although he was beginning to think he did. "The purring... does it sound familiar?"

"I don't know. It just sounds like a cat."

He looked at Emily for a long time. She sighed under his gaze.

"It sounds like Hider," she said finally.

Scott nodded. "He's come back to us."

"But why?" Emily's eyes welled, springs long dry replenished now, suddenly, in the eleventh hour.

"Because we cared for him when no one else would," said Jacob.

"But he cried and cried by the door, and we didn't let him in!"

"Yes... and we always went out to see him instead. It was enough. And now he's finally inside. That's all we really need to know. And I haven't sneezed once."

The room, suddenly warm, brought sleep quickly, and as it took them both they felt the mattress shift as something small and soft lay down between them. And they knew, as sleep gave way to dreams, that for all the winters that followed they would never feel the sting of ice or the oppression of gray skies again.

"Welcome," Scott murmured, rolling over.

"Welcome home," Emily said, and took his hand.

Armistice Day

He was 109 years old, and breathed like a brittle leaf harried by cold wind. Lungs rattled, moth-wing ears twitched, and hair like spider silk downed the crown of his head as dreams roved his mind like trenchant guards.

"Mr. Farnon is fading." A hospital attendant named Ainsworth looked at the doctor's chart by the foot of the old man's bed and clucked his tongue. His on-duty partner, Brian Holdman, crossed his arms in the doorway but did not approach. Behind Holdman the halls were shadowed and silenced by midnight, a distant life support machine the only sound that broke the Witching Hour's calm. Even so, Ainsworth felt uneasy, as if some terrible catastrophe was about to come crashing down on them like an irrepressible wave.

"Come away from there," Holdman said. "He's not to be bothered."

Slowly, looking back over his shoulder several times, Ainsworth did as Holdman said. He closed the door quietly behind them as they left.

In the attendant lounge, Ainsworth took a sip of his Coke and shook his head. "The reporters have been gathering like vultures. Just this morning he granted an interview, can you believe it? *Newsweek*, I think. But that took it out of him. Doc Jordan said no more, but I don't think he could give another anyway."

Holdman snorted through a bite of ham sandwich. "I don't see what the big deal is. He's old, and he's going to die, and that's the way of things. That happens to lots of people without all this fuss."

"But he's the *last*," said Ainsworth. "The final one. Fourteen *million* men fought in World War I, and they're all gone now. All except him."

"I know, I know, you keep saying that. It had to happen sometime."

Ainsworth shook his head. For a moment he seriously considered punching Holdman in the eye. That, he figured, would get through to him better than anything else he could do. But instead he said, very quietly, "I want you to imagine something. Can you do that, Holdman?"

Holdman muttered something unintelligible.

"Close your eyes," said Ainsworth, and closed his own without waiting to see if Holdman complied.

"I want you to picture," he continued, "Yankee Stadium on a packed fall day. Now imagine *two hundred* packed Yankee Stadiums. That's how many people fought in World War I."

Silence from Holdman.

"Now imagine the front lines of the trenches, like Wilfred Owen described in his poems."

"Who?" asked Holdman.

"Imagine 'No-Man's Land,' bodies rotting in the sun and rain, yellow pools of toxic sludge filling up around them, men watching the carrion birds from deep-dug trenches laced with barbed wire, and machine guns popping dull and thick without any rhythm, incessantly, all day and into the night. The charges. The disease. Biplanes scattering men like ants…Mr. Farnon saw it all. When he dies …"

Ainsworth opened his eyes. Holdman was gone.

He walked back down to Mr. Farnon's room and stood outside the closed door for a long time.

When he dies, Ainsworth continued silently, *fourteen million men die with him a second time. Every single one of them becomes a second-hand story*

... or, worse, nothing. Not even a name in a faded ledger. He keeps them alive, all of them, in that egg-shell fragile body. Even the ones he never saw or met. Because he breathed their air, drank their drinks, shared their world...

When he dies, Ainsworth thought on, *a generation winks out of existence. When his eyes close for the last time, no one will ever again look into eyes that saw the first tanks trundle across the blasted fields of the Somme. When his mouth shuts for good, no one will ever again hear a voice that shouted up at the Red Baron as he flashed overhead, a hated, dazzling streak of lethal elegance.*

He opened the door to Mr. Farnon's room quietly, carefully, and sat down gingerly on the edge of the old man's bed.

Ainsworth wanted to ask Mr. Farnon a question. Very badly, he wanted that. As far as he knew, no reporter had ever asked it before. Even if one had, Ainsworth didn't care. He wanted to hear it from the man himself.

The question he wanted to ask was, "What was it like at the eleventh minute of the eleventh hour of the eleventh day of the eleventh month? When you were eighteen years old and the guns went silent?"

But he hadn't the heart to wake Mr. Farnon. There are some lines that even the deepest desires shouldn't cross.

Without a word, Ainsworth stood up and left the room, silent as a moth.

* * * * *

Just before dawn, Holdman popped his head in the door of the public bathroom where Ainsworth was washing his hands.

"Your friend just bought it," he said simply, and ducked out again.

Ainsworth turned off the water and waited for the last drop to fall from the faucet. Then he left the bathroom and walked over to Mr. Farnon's room a short way down the hall.

No one had arrived yet except for one doctor, who was now at the main desk making some hurried phone calls in a low voice.

Holdman stood beside Ainsworth and they both looked into the room, now completely shadowed, and at Mr. Farnon, now completely still.

Neither man said anything for a long time. Finally, Ainsworth spoke.

"Hear that?" he asked quietly.

Holdman stared at him like he was crazy. "No, man, I don't hear anything."

"Silence," Ainsworth said. Somewhere deep, a part of him had expected fourteen million voices to raise shouts against time, a thunderous barrage.

Holdman walked away, shaking his head.

"Complete and utter silence," Ainsworth added.

"I wonder…" he finished, "…if *that's* what it was like?"

Hollow's End

The forest stretched across long-abandoned fields and deep red-rust valleys. It hedged back roads leading to lonely whitewashed houses and dipped through night streams that inhaled leaves and exhaled cold. As the sun sank and the day died, icy wind flowed down from the high October sky. Boughs creaked and clattered, a desolate cacophony that roused owls to flight and sent mice scurrying for shelter. And in a sunken field between two hills on the outskirts of a nestled country town, all darkness was doubled, all creatures red-eyed.

In one small house at the end of a thin dirt lane at the far end of that town, James Holt, ten years old, listened to the wind rattle skeletal bonewood trees and felt his blood run cold.

"James?" His father stepped into his bedroom and looked around. "Hey, champ, where are you?"

"Under the bed," a soft voice replied.

Mr. Holt sat down on the bed while James crawled out. "Mom's been calling you down to dinner for ten minutes. She's going hoarse! What's the problem?"

"Nothing." At that moment an especially strong gust of wind gibbered through distant tree trunks and slammed against the windowpanes, insistent, clamoring. James gasped, jumped, and grabbed his father's arm.

Mr. Holt smiled. "It's the wind… that's all, champ. Nothing but the wind."

"No," James said urgently. "It's not the wind—It's the *hollow*."

Gently, Mr. Holt removed his arm from his son's tight grip. "You still scared of the hollow?"

James nodded, wide-eyed and pale. "Even the wind is scared of it. The wind don't scream until it reaches the hollow."

"But you're home, safe and sound! Bright lights, warm blankets, good food. Speaking of that… come on down for dinner. Mom's pork chops are getting cold."

James sighed and followed him down the stairs.

"Oh, hey!" His father turned. "I'm taking off early tomorrow. Wanna pick pumpkins after school?"

"Yeah, sure! But… but the pumpkin patch is through the hollow, Dad. You know that."

"You went last year. And the year before. We do it *every* year."

Mr. Holt looked at his son's quavering lip and sighed.

"We'll go while the sun's still high in the sky." And under his breath: "*Also* like we do every year."

* * * * *

Even by day, the hollow was a dark place. Trees grew thicker in its cool depths, down in the gully between the steep hills of Old Man Turner's far fields. Ancient trunks rose from loam made thick by a thousand years of fallen autumn leaves. Cobwebs laced across skeletal branches and strange things howled from the shadows of the inner forest where no one ever stepped. Rumor had it there were stone cottages lost among those shifting boughs, unseen since before the Civil War. In there, ghosts held court with murderers, and things that shouldn't walk crept and slithered on the far edge of sideway sight.

"C'mon, Dad, let's hurry."

The thin dirt path cut through the trees like a scar. James walked it like a tightrope.

His father followed behind, pulling a small wagon. "There's nothing to worry about, you know. I keep telling you but you don't listen."

James sighed. "You haven't heard the stories."

"Ha! I've heard 'em all! This place is older than Grandpa by five hundred years. It looked the same when I was young."

"OK then, you ever been deep in those trees?" A branch cracked in the distance and James shot a wide-eyed stare across the orange and red curtain of leaves.

His father shook his head. "Never. When I was your age we was scared, too. Then I grew up and never saw the point. Here we are."

They stepped into a small, wheat-sifted glade beside an ancient, towering oak. Left over from some long-dead settler's reclaimed fields, the pumpkin patch grew in coiled russet luxury beneath the lowest branches, its heavy orange blooms shockingly bright in the fading autumn sun.

Together, eager, they started the search.

But finding the *right* pumpkins took longer than expected. James wanted a thin, tall one and a fat, squat one – no rotten spots, no green streaks. By the time that was done, the sun, much to his surprised horror, had already begun to set.

"We'd better hurry," he told his father as he raced to load the pumpkins onto the cart.

"What could happen? If some ol' ghost comes after you, I'll knock it on its head."

James didn't look convinced as they started back. By day, the hollow was a dark place. By night, even by *twilight*, it was a living shadow, a force to ice his spine and darken his dreams. As long as he could remember, its proximity to his house had impressed him... that something so mysterious, so *dangerous*, could exist so close to his life.

"Nothing to worry about," his father added as they strode quickly through the encroaching gloom—James in front and impatient; he lingering behind, enjoying the evening.

It happened just moments later.

A freezing night wind rustled through dead leaves, bringing with it a cry to convulse stomachs and shudder spines. James stopped dead, heart rabbit-pounding, sitting prey to whatever might come.

"That sounded like a wolf," he whispered.

His father shook his head. "There aren't wolves around here. Not since Grandpa was a kid and they killed off the last of them. A dog. Old Man Turner's hound."

The howl rose and fell, buffeted by currents of air, distinctly close.

Then it faded, ceased, and silence settled… followed quickly by laughter, faint and distant. A child's voice, somewhere in the dark trees where children never ventured.

"It's the Crying Ghost!" James hissed, grabbing his father's hand tight.

"Nothing but a cat," Mr. Holt reassured him, but James knew better.

Why, he thought, *is my father so blind?*

* * * * *

Every day after supper the children gathered in the park. Between kick-the-can and catch, they huddled around red picnic tables and rope-board swing sets. Every year, when the first skeleton cutouts appeared in windows and the first Halloween Trees bloomed in yards, their conversations turned to the same thing.

"Grandpa says that sometimes a boy wearing old-fashioned clothes can be seen tramping around among the trees. Always at dusk. If you try following him, he leads you deeper and deeper in, always a dozen steps ahead, until he reaches an old stone well. Then he turns, and you finally see his face, only he don't got no eyes. And he tries to grab you and drag you down into that ol' well. Cause that's where he died a hundred years ago."

Ed Graybill nodded his head, confident in the truth of his story. The other children murmured, entranced, wide-eyed. James felt cold sweat bead his brow.

Brian Lumley took up Ed's torch. "I heard there was a p'fessor who went hunting a rare spider back in there. Wanted it for a study.

So he went lookin' deep in, where no one goes, an' found one of those old stone huts from back before the Revolution. It was as picture-perfect as the day it was left empty, only *everything* inside was full of spider webs. Floor to ceiling, corner to corner. An' in the fireplace was the spider he was lookin' for, only it was big as a dog, an' all gray and furry, an' in its webs was all kinds of things—birds an' rats an' rabbits an' squirrels. An' it made a start for him, so that p'fessor stumbled out, an' when he came home his eyes was all wide an' starey an' *he never spoke again.*"

Murmurs. Then Sarah Fuller said, "If he never spoke again, how we know *what* he saw?"

Brian rolled his eyes. "Cause he wrote it *down*, silly! An' that's why you don't see many animals down in that hollow, an' why so many's pets go missing."

"You ain't gonna have to worry about *that* much longer."

Everyone turned. One of the high school boys, Pete Gifford, stood beside the picnic table, hands in jeans, chewing a plug of tobacco.

"Whatta ya mean, Pete?" Brian asked.

He grinned, displaying stained teeth. "I mean that starting tomorrow, Heinz Construction is gonna bulldoze the hollow clear away. It's got a new owner, and he wants to plant on that land."

The children looked at one another in shocked amazement.

"They... they can't do *that*," Ed Graybill exclaimed.

Pete Gifford spit tobacco and straddled the picnic bench, forcing everyone else over. "They can do any damn thing they want... and what's more, I'll be running one of the dozers! After all these years, we're gonna get to the root of all those dumb stories—then shovel over and bury every last trace of 'em."

He smirked, spat, got up, and loped away.

No one said anything for a long time. Then a few chimed up:

"I wanna be there to see *that!*"

"It'll never happen... the hollow won't *let* it happen."

"I wonder what they'll *find?*"

"Grownups ruin *everything*."

But James kept silent, though his mind was a turbulent riot of joy and relief.

He smiled discreetly. And when it came time for dinner, he whistled past the entrance of the hollow without a second thought, stopping only long enough to notice the gleaming row of hulking chrome bulldozers lined up and ready to destroy.

"Your days," he murmured at the ancient trees, "are numbered."

* * * * *

Gone, he thought that night, no longer *under* his bed but *in* it.

Not yet, but *soon.*

Gone soon, he thought again, and stared up at the ceiling in the moonlit dark. Soon was close enough.

After a long ten minutes he rolled over. *So quiet,* he thought. The wind blew, rattling the window, but it didn't scream or cry. Far off, a howl echoed faintly over the hills—most definitely Old Man Turner's hound, and certainly not a wolf.

James rolled over on his other side, twisting beneath his blankets, then kicked them off in frustration. The night felt dull. His mind chased itself in circles.

He slipped out of bed and walked over to the window, wide awake even as midnight tolled downstairs on the grandfather clock. He looked out over the milky fields and sighed.

He raised his eyes farther. Beyond the fields, past the cornhusks, a place loomed where no moonlight had ever dared fall.

Tonight, however, the hollow was bathed in faint silver light that softened its shadows and reflected the great steel shovels poised on the brink of its earthen skin. James stared at it for a long time, breath even and calm, face warm against the cool windowpane. Then, bored and confused, he returned to bed.

Two long hours later he sat up with a start, still wide awake, a recent voice now replaying in his mind as a surprising truth: *Grownups ruin everything…*

Shortly thereafter, had anyone been looking, they would have seen a small figure in red checkered pajamas running across the darkened fields.

* * * * *

"Cut clean through, every one!"

Ed Graybill nodded his head, confident in the truth of his story. "All the gas lines, all the brake lines. All the tires slashed, too. And sugar in all the tanks! Pete Gifford is *pissed!*"

Excited murmurs rose and fell around the red picnic table.

Brian Lumley took up Ed's torch. "They say Heinz Construction's gonna walk. The job's off, at least 'til spring. The hollow's not going anywhere for now."

There was a long pause. No one spoke.

Then, hesitantly, someone piped in, "I heard there's a madman who lives in there, way back in a hidden cave. He escaped from an asylum back in the fifties, an'—"

Later that night a storm rolled through town and across the distant farms. The wind shrieked. Distant trees moaned. A wolf howled.

And under his bed, scared to death, James Holt shivered, smiling a jack o' lantern grin.

About the Author

Gregory Miller was born in State College, Pennsylvania in 1978. His short fiction and poetry have appeared in a number of national publications. His first novel, *Big Cicadas*, was published in 2003 and his first collection of poetry, *Four Autumns,* in 2005. In 2004 he served as a freelance consultant for Houghton Mifflin's *The Lord of the Rings* online curriculum guide. A high school English teacher, he currently lives in Pittsburgh with his wife, Vera, and son, Samuel.

About the Illustrator

John Randall York was born in Texas and grew up playing and working in a small zoo where his father was the director. He loves ghost stories, old horror movies and illustrations from the middle 20th century. He also enjoys writing songs and playing guitar. John has designed giftware for S & D Limoges, Lenox China, The Hamilton Collection, Fitz&Floyd, and Faroy. His artwork is available on his website, www.johnrandallyork.com. *Scaring the Crows: 21 Tales for Noon or Midnight* is his first adventure in book illustration. He currently lives in Tyler, Texas with his wife and three cats.

VISIT
STONEGARDEN.NET PUBLISHING ONLINE!

You can find us at: www.stonegardenbooks.com

News and Upcoming Titles
New titles and reader favorites are featured each month, along with information on our upcoming titles.

Author Info
Author bios, blogs and links to their personal websites.

Contests and Other Fun Stuff
A forum to keep in touch with your favorite authors, autographed copies and more!

Breinigsville, PA USA
28 May 2010
238921BV00001B/1/P